3

THE CASE OF THE RUNAWAY GIRL

THE CHRONICLE OF A LADY DETECTIVE

K.B. OWEN

CHAPTER 1

CHICAGO, JANUARY 1887

*T*rouble comes in threes, as they say, and that certainly proved true for me one particular day in early January. My friend and housemate, Cassie Leigh, was tucked into her bed with a bout of bronchitis, so we were already shorthanded when our ancient coal stove decided to drop its rusted belly of hot coals —and the charred chicken carcass, to boot—upon the kitchen floor and catch it on fire.

Our maid, Sadie, grabbed the dustpan. "What a mess!"

"Such a good-sized chicken, too," the widow Hodges, one of our lodgers, *tsk*ed. "I suppose it's irrecoverable, Miss Hamilton?"

The lady was a good eater, but obviously even she had her limits.

My answer was to rummage through the larder and pull out what was left of yesterday's ham, pickled beets, and cold biscuits. With Cassie sick and several vacancies at our boarding house, there were only four of us dining tonight. It should suffice. But what to do about affording another stove was the bigger problem.

We were finishing supper when the bell rang. I didn't know it at the time, but problem number three was at my front door.

The burnt odor lingered as I closed the kitchen and dining room doors behind me and hurried down the hall. If this was a prospective lodger, I doubt we would make a good impression.

Nonetheless, I smoothed my skirt and tugged at my cuffs before pulling open the front door.

The tall, lean man standing before me was all too familiar. And most unwelcome.

"Frank! What on earth brings you here?"

My estranged husband, Frank Wynch, narrowed his eyes at the sharpness of my tone. "It's urgent, Pen," he muttered. "Pinkerton business." He jerked a thumb toward the two ladies standing behind him. One was a petite, dark-haired girl wearing a rumpled school uniform and carrying a valise that had seen better days. She looked barely old enough to be out of pigtails. At her elbow was a sensibly shod, prim-mouthed woman. She appeared to be close to my age—mid-thirtyish—though the heavy-rimmed spectacles may have aged her.

He waved a hand in my direction. "Ladies, this is Mrs.—"

"*Miss* Hamilton," I interrupted, before Frank could introduce me as his wife. It was a complication I did not wish to explain to strangers. I opened the door wider to let them in.

The girl sniffed the air suspiciously. "Something's burning!" Her voice was high-pitched and strident, not in the least resembling the subdued tones of an educated young miss. The woman gave her a reproving nudge.

"Something *was* burning," I answered, with as much dignity as I could muster. "We will be more comfortable in the parlor. Mr. Wynch and I will join you in a moment. First door on your left."

I waited until they were out of earshot. "You know I do not care for you showing up at my house," I hissed. "You could have sent a message to meet you at the office tomorrow morning."

"There was no time." He nudged the front door closed with his foot and gave me a warm, lingering look. "I haven't seen you in ages. You're looking well, my dear. And you are wearing your hair differently. Most becoming."

In spite of myself, I raised a self-conscious hand to tuck a blonde strand into my loose-waved chignon. The man had not lost his sweet-tongued, devilish ways. "It has only been a year since we worked together on the Comstock case," I retorted mildly.

And there would be other occasions, this being one of them— whatever *this* was. It was the price one paid for being among the few female investigators in Mr. Pinkerton's agency. But I didn't have to like it.

He moved closer and took my hand. "I still miss you, Pen. Every day. Did you know it's been four years? Four years since we've lived together as man and wife."

"I am well aware of that." I looked into the hazel eyes that regarded me so earnestly. There was no denying he was a handsome man, when sober. Undoubtedly the ladies of his acquaintance sighed over those heavily lashed eyes, the strong jaw, the six-foot, lanky frame. Not many men are taller than I... Was it getting warm in here?

I snatched my hand away as our two guests turned at the parlor door to look back, no doubt wondering what kept us. The girl smothered a giggle behind her glove.

"Miss me all you like," I snapped, "but keep your hands to yourself, if you please." I hurried to catch up to our guests, Frank following.

"Whatever you say, my dear," he murmured.

The woman perched upon the settee beside the fire. She was a study in ladylike composure as she adjusted her steel-rimmed spectacles and smoothed her gloves. The girl, however, prowled the room. She paced from hearth to desk to window, once stopping to push the curtain aside and look out, although at this time of evening it was too dark to see much beyond the lamp post at the street corner. Her entire aspect—pale, twitchy, eyes wide and alert—bespoke the restless strain of a captive.

"Miss Pelley," the woman said sharply, "you will sit beside me."

The girl complied, skirting Frank with a wary look. Not that there was anything especially menacing about his demeanor at the moment. He seemed perfectly at his ease, in fact, propping his foot upon the hearth fender and leaning a shoulder against the mantel. But after years of working with my husband, I was well-acquainted with the languid pose that belied his sharp attentiveness. All of his focus was upon this girl, and she knew it.

The silence lengthened.

I looked from girl to woman, and lastly to Frank. "Would someone do me the kindness of telling me who you people are and what this is about?"

The woman leaned forward. "I am Miss Rotenberg, head-mistress of the Chicago Ladies' Seminary. This is Miss Claudine Pelley, a pupil at our institution, although her future at the school is currently in doubt."

The aforementioned Miss Pelley threw herself back against the cushions in a sulk, muttering something that sounded like *old rutabaga*.

My lips twitched as I gathered her import. Although Miss Rotenberg in no way resembled the vegetable, the similarity to her name was irresistible. It seemed that every generation devised disparaging nicknames for its betters.

As expected of any headmistress worth her salt, Miss Roten-berg declined to dignify the remark, to the girl's obvious disap-pointment. "Should Miss Pelley not be sent to her room while we discuss the arrangements?" she asked.

I flashed a look at Frank. "*Her room?*"

He ignored me and pulled the cord to ring for Sadie. Consid-ering the maid's prompt arrival and the cap askew upon her head, she'd no doubt been hunched over the keyhole. Not that I was in a position to disapprove. I'd done the same myself at countless doors over the years.

"Yes?" she asked, surreptitiously attempting to set the cap to rights.

Before I could say a thing, Frank pointed at Claudine Pelley. "The young lady is staying the night."

Sadie stiffened. She knew who paid her wages, meager as they were. She also knew Frank and wasn't about to show him any courtesies. She turned to me. "Your instructions, Miss Hamilton?"

Frank glared at her back.

Bless the girl. No one addressed me by my married name of *Wynch* while I was mistress here. "You may take Miss Pelley up to the general's old room for now, until we settle things here."

Miss Pelley got up with an aggrieved sigh.

Frank waggled a finger in her direction. "Stay there until we tell you otherwise. *Do you understand?*"

She scowled and gave him a wide berth as she followed Sadie out.

"You were rather sharp with her," I said.

Frank sat and stretched his legs toward the fire. "I don't care to chase her through the city again. She got away from me twice."

No wonder he was annoyed. To be bested by a mere child... I turned my amused snort into a polite cough. "Better start from the beginning. Tell me about the girl."

He waved a tired hand toward the headmistress. "You know her better than I."

"Of course." Miss Rotenberg sat up straighter, if that were possible. "Claudine Pelley was admitted to our academy as a boarding pupil last August. She's a bright young lady, a quick learner, but she is exceedingly stubborn. She does not like to follow rules. Naturally, such an inclination has brought restrictions down upon her head on several occasions. I imagine that is why she ran away."

"How old is she?" I asked.

"Fifteen. She looks younger, I grant you," the lady added, no doubt noting my surprise. "She is slightly built."

"And she doesn't *act* in a mature fashion," Frank growled.

Miss Rotenberg grimaced. "To be fair, she has not had training in proper comportment. Her education covered the three *R*s at a local country school, but her father—she is motherless—permitted her to run wild on the family farm. We have tried to catch her up. As you can see, I have not been entirely successful. Before we discovered her missing the day before yesterday, I had considered sending her home for good. She is a disruptive influence."

I turned to Frank. "How did you come to be involved?"

"Miss Rotenberg is a family friend of William Pinkerton," Frank said. "She asked us to find the girl, rather than call the police."

The headmistress twisted her gloved hands in her lap. "We cannot afford that sort of notoriety. For a premier ladies' school such as ours, reputation is paramount."

"Where did you find her?"

"At the home of the Zaleski family," Frank said, "not far from the school. Miss Pelley is friends with Anna, a daughter of the same age. The family was debating what to do next when I showed up. That was the easiest part of taking charge of the girl." He scowled. "At one point today, after we left the telegraph office, she slipped away amid the throng at a corner bus stop. When we finally caught up to her, we took a cab and headed to Pinkerton's office. But then she jumped out at a congested intersection." He shook his head, equal parts frustration and grudging admiration. "She timed it perfectly. Our vehicle was closely hemmed in on both sides. She was small enough to slip out and knew perfectly well that I was not. By the time I tracked her down again, Pinkerton had left for the night, so we came here."

"You mentioned going to the telegraph office," I said. "I take it her father has been notified?"

Miss Rotenberg shifted in her seat. "He recently left for California for railroad work. The only other relation she has is a great-uncle and his family. They are in charge of her until the father returns."

"Well then"—I waved an impatient hand—"you have notified the great-uncle?"

"He's in Washington," Frank said. "We haven't heard back yet."

"Washington?" I echoed. "The territory or the capitol?"

"The capitol," he said. "Claudine Pelley's great-uncle is Shelby Moore Cullom, one of Illinois' U.S. senators. It would have been a simple matter to take her to his house in Springfield, but we discovered Cullom closed it up and went back to Washington last week, after the New Year's holiday. He and his family reside there during the legislative session."

Cullom. I don't follow politics much, but even I had heard of him. He'd notably begun his career as a junior counsel for Abraham Lincoln during that man's days as a practicing attorney in Springfield. Cullom went on to serve in the state legislature, then as governor, and now in the United States Senate. Even his adversaries respected him.

No wonder the headmistress had not wanted the police brought in. To lose a pupil was bad enough, but to lose the grand-niece of a locally famous politician...she may as well be growing those rutabagas. "What do you think the senator will say?" I asked Miss Rotenberg.

Her jaw tensed. "He will want her returned to the school, but that is impossible. Short of locking her up, I cannot guarantee she won't run away again. Besides, her presence undermines our discipline. Some of the younger girls copy her hoydenish ways."

"She could easily run away from here," I pointed out. "I cannot keep her a prisoner."

"We should have Cullom's answer tomorrow," Frank said. "I'll stay here in the meantime, just in case."

7

I stifled a sigh. My estranged husband sleeping under my roof was not conducive to my peace of mind. "And then?"

He shrugged. "We'll escort her wherever the senator instructs, and that will be the end of it. She'll be someone else's problem after that."

The house was settling down for the night. Miss Rotenberg had been put in a cab, Sadie had checked on the now-sleeping girl, and Frank was bedding down in the parlor with the door to the hallway left open, in case the young lady was of a mind to slip out the front door. The back door of the kitchen was locked, and I had possession of the key. Short of her climbing out a window, all was secure.

I tapped quietly on Cassie's door and opened it at the sound of a muffled "Come in."

My friend was propped up on pillows, sipping water from a tumbler. Although her skin was sallow and she looked much too thin, she was clear-eyed and held the glass without a tremor. All good signs.

"Feeling better?"

She nodded. "The druggist's tonic has worked wonders. I should be back on my feet tomorrow."

"I wouldn't rush to get up too soon, dear. Sadie and I have everything under control."

Cassie's grunt turned into a coughing spasm. "That's not what I hear," she said, when she'd recovered her breath. "Mrs. Hodges told me of the disaster with the stove. How are we to possibly afford another?"

"I may have a case. That should bring in enough for something secondhand." I told her of Frank's arrival with clients in tow.

Cassie frowned. "I don't like the idea of him being back in your life, Pen. Did you lock up the liquor?"

"It's not worth protecting a dusty bottle of port and half a flask of sherry. Besides, he has sworn off the stuff." Though last year, during the Comstock case, his resolve had faltered.

"You know he's made similar pledges in the past," Cassie pointed out.

All too true. It had taken me a long time to stop believing his promises and finally show him the door. The delay had nearly cost me my life, and I had lost a babe in the process. Never again.

I took a breath. "No matter, he won't be here long." I got up and smoothed the covers. "Once we have our instructions regarding Claudine Pelley, I will accompany her where she needs to go and collect my fee. That will be an end of it. Frank may not even need to come along, should the young lady decide to behave herself." I dearly hoped that would be the case.

"What is this girl like?" Cassie asked, leaning forward as I fluffed her pillows.

"She's a little thing, looks much younger than her fifteen years. Sulky. Stubborn. Atrocious manners. Her schoolmistress says she's quick and clever, though, which I believe. She led Frank on a merry chase through the city and slipped away from him twice."

Cassie smiled. "I like her already."

I grimaced. "I'll have my hands full with this one."

My prediction came true sooner than I expected.

CHAPTER 2

*T*he sound awoke me around four in the morning. I sat up and listened, wondering if in my half-sleep I had dreamt the soft *chink* on glass.

The sound did not repeat, but now I heard the creak of floorboards near the stairwell landing. I had no doubt Miss Pelley was on the move.

I shrugged on my robe. My slippers were nowhere in sight, drat it. Barefoot it was, then.

I'm not sure what made me decide to follow the girl in secret rather than confront her and order her back to bed. Something told me she wouldn't be alone. Perhaps it was the tap of the glass —a bit of gravel tossed up to her nearby casement? I also remembered, when they first arrived, the girl pulling aside the curtain to look out the parlor window. What—or whom—was she looking for? The possibility of strangers lurking near our windows made me uneasy. I had to get to the bottom of this.

I passed the parlor door, still ajar. Frank was sprawled on the settee, feet dangling over the edge, snoring slightly beneath the afghan. So much for keeping watch. Perhaps he *had* dipped into the sherry. That was a question for later. If I wanted to catch Claudine Pelley, there was no time even to rouse him.

The front door was closed but no longer on the latch. I slipped out quietly, wincing as my bare feet encountered the cold steps.

By the curb was an expressman's cart, the horse snuffling in the chill air. The girl, fully dressed and carrying her valise, whispered earnestly to a short, stocky young man who stood beside the horse. They embraced. He took her bag and tossed it into the cart.

What was this? A tryst? An elopement?

I reached them just as the youth was helping boost her up.

"Where do you think you are going, Miss Pelley?" As my attire was undignified in the extreme, I made up for it with a stern tone and glowering look.

They froze, the young man staring at me with widened eyes. Not that I could blame him. It isn't every day one is accosted by a barefoot, irregularly clad woman out on the street in the pre-dawn hours.

The girl recovered her composure first, ignoring me and continuing to hoist herself into the cart.

Well, the little miss was going nowhere without a driver. I fixed my wrath upon the youth. I leaned in close, towering over him by an easy six inches. "And who might you be, young man? What are your intentions toward the young lady?"

He shrank back. "Ah'm...well, I... She didn' want ta be here no more." He jerked a thumb toward the girl.

"Don't pay her any mind, Eddie," she called, glaring at me for good measure. "Let's go."

He shifted his cap to scratch his head, looking back and forth between us. Duller than a disused hoe, this one was.

I clutched my robe more closely as the cold seeped through the fabric. "If you take her away, I shall call the police, and you will be charged with kidnapping."

He held up his hands defensively. "I ain't a kidnapper! Look here, I'll jes' go. I don't want no trouble, ma'am."

I'd had enough of shivering outdoors in my sleeping attire. "Well, then—Eddie, is it? We must have a talk in my house first. As the one charged with Miss Pelley's safekeeping at the moment, I deserve an explanation of what is going on. After that, you may go."

He sighed in resignation and secured the horse to the post hitch. The girl stared down at the youth in disbelief.

I hid a smile. "Coming, Miss Pelley?" I led the way as he helped her down.

As we approached the front porch, movement in the shrubbery along the alley side caught my attention. The sound suggested something larger than a night creature. I swung around for a better look, but soft footfalls in the alley told me that whoever it was had fled. If I had not been listening carefully, I would have missed even that.

I frowned. Who had been watching us? None of my neighbors would be so surreptitious. They were more likely to step out and chastise me for disturbing their sleep.

Well, there was nothing to be done about it tonight.

Frank was in the hall putting on his shoes when we came through the door. "Who is *this*?" he thundered, pointing at the boy.

"I was just about to determine that," I answered, prodding both young people past Frank and down the hall to the kitchen, which was the warmest part of the house and the only room with a banked fire at this hour of the morning. He turned as if to follow us, but I put a hand on his arm. "Let me handle it. You go home."

"But she may try to escape again," he said.

I resisted the urge to point out that his presence hadn't deterred the young lady the first time around. I had neither the time nor the energy for a quarrel. "She is dependent upon her male companion for transportation. I believe I have frightened him sufficiently that he will not offer her further aid for the time being."

He sighed and turned to go.

"While you're out there, check the grounds and the alley. Someone was lurking nearby. I couldn't see who."

He raised an eyebrow, but to his credit he accepted my statement at face value. We had worked together on enough cases for him to know I wasn't prone to nerves or an overactive imagination. "All right. Lock the door behind me. I'll be back later, as soon as Cullom sends a reply."

The milkman had already left our two quarts of milk outside on the back stoop. I carried them in and filled three glasses, then opened a tin of ginger crisps and set it on the table.

The youngsters quietly nibbled on the cookies while I stoked the fire and turned up the lamps. Fortunately, the smell of smoke had dissipated, and the room was soon comfortably warm. I drank my milk and watched them for a time. Eddie was compactly built, with a soft, baby-hair mustache typical of a youth of perhaps sixteen or seventeen years of age. He certainly had an appetite to match. I'd already refilled his glass twice, and half of the cookies were gone.

Claudine Pelley toyed with her napkin, her mind obviously elsewhere, but at least her face no longer held a harried look. Both were calmer, more relaxed.

Milk and cookies. I never imagined quieting clients with something so banal. Perhaps I should add that to my list of basic equipment, along with my lockpicks and derringer.

Of course, Frank being gone might have had something to do with it, too.

"More milk, Eddie?" I held up the bottle.

"No thanks, ma'am," he said, wiping his mouth on his sleeve.

"How long have you known Miss Pelley?" I asked.

He glanced over at the girl. "All my life, I guess. Our farms were next to each other."

When he didn't add anything more—it seemed a great effort for him to share even that bit—I prodded further. "But you don't live on a farm anymore, correct? You must live here in town, nearby." Then I remembered something Frank had said. "Eddie, is your last name Zaleski, by any chance?"

"Yes'm," he said.

More silence.

I turned to the girl. "Miss Pelley, are you going to leave all the explaining to your companion? If so, we may be here a while."

Was that a ghost of a smile I saw?

"Eddie's family had to give up their farm a few years ago," she began, "and move to the city. His father works in the paper mill, and Eddie's apprenticing there, too." The boy made a move as if to add something, but she held up a hand.

"Your headmistress believes you ran away because you don't care for rules and resented the discipline. Is her assessment correct?"

The girl shrugged. "I am always doing something wrong." She altered her voice to imitate Miss Rotenberg. "'Talk softly, dear. Don't fidget. Don't argue. Don't cross your legs.'" She sighed. "So many *don'ts*. Can you imagine boys being told those things?"

Although she had a point, I was not about to address the inequities behind what governs ladylike behavior. "Running away from school will not change what is expected of you in adult society."

She grimaced. "I know. But there was more to it than that. I hadn't a single friend. I missed Anna."

I nodded in understanding. "Ah, yes. Eddie's sister."

She stiffened in surprise. "That's right. How did—? Oh. *He* told you."

"Indeed." Wanting to steer her thoughts away from Frank, I quickly added, "Do you think your great-uncle would permit you to stay with the Zaleskis for now?" That would give the senator time to find another school for Miss Pelley. Did her friend Anna still attend school? Perhaps Miss Pelley could accompany her for a while.

The girl exchanged a glance with Eddie, who shook his head in my direction. "We've got trouble of our own, miss. It's best she not get mixed up in it." He rubbed a hand across his head, leaving the dark hair mussed and standing on end.

When he said nothing more, the young lady explained. "Eddie's pa was taken away by the police a few days ago, just before I got there."

"The police! Why?"

"They're questioning him about who else was involved in the bomb attack at Haymarket Square," she said. "Mr. Zaleski's active in the union, you see, and knew Albert Parsons, one of the men convicted. The police think there were more involved."

"But the trial was last summer. Months ago," I said. "The men have all been sentenced."

"There's still a lot o' bad feeling 'bout the unions," Eddie said. "Some think the union folks are nothing but agitators, off makin' bombs with the anarchists." He gave a derisive snort.

The boy felt strongly about the subject, it seemed. That was the longest pair of sentences he'd uttered since being here. I shook myself and turned my attention back to the girl. "So, Miss Pelley, if you weren't planning to return to stay with the Zaleskis, where were you and Eddie heading when I stopped you?"

The girl hesitated. "I'm keeping my plans to myself. If Uncle Shelby sends me back to the school, I will *not* go."

"I grant you that he may try to do so, but Miss Rotenberg herself will recommend against such a course."

The girl sat up straight. "Really?" Then she blew out a noisy breath. "She'd be happy to be rid of me, I suppose. I can't say I blame her."

I grimaced. "From what I gather, you *were* rather horrid."

Eddie's mouth dropped open.

I half expected the girl to go into the sulks again over my bald remark but instead, she threw back her head and laughed. "Fair enough, Miss—it's Hamilton, isn't it? You're right. I *have* been horrible. But I am still not telling you my plans."

Well, at least she was honest. I tried a different approach. "What would you *want* your uncle to propose you do?"

The girl's expression turned wistful. "I would like to go to Uncle Shelby's house in Washington."

Eddie gave a vigorous nod. "That's what you were gonna do, anyhow."

She glared. "Eddie!"

"Ah'm sorry." He spread his heads in a helpless gesture. "A'least I didn' tell her about Anna going with ya—" He clamped both hands over his mouth.

I smothered a chuckle. "You and Anna were simply going to hop a train to Washington and arrive at your uncle's doorstep, without notice of any kind? How would you pay for tickets, or were you planning to stow away?" Young people are a cheeky lot.

The girl rolled her eyes. "Nothing like *that*. I have money saved from the allowance Uncle Shelby provides. Anna and I were going to buy tickets for the eight twenty train this morning to Pittsburgh. We would send a telegram from there, when it was too late for Uncle Shelby to order me back. Then we'd take the B&O line from Pittsburgh to Washington and hire a cab to his house."

While her plan had the merit of aforethought, and providing herself with a companion showed some prudence, I shuddered to think of the two young ladies traveling without adult supervision. "Does Anna's mother know you were planning this?"

Eddie chimed in with a nod. "Ma thinks it's best for Anna to leave so the police don't lock her up, too. We expect they will be coming for all of us."

I sat back and considered the problem. Assuming Cullom was willing, it made sense for the young ladies to leave town and stay with his family in Washington for a while. The dark figure lurking by my house troubled me. Was someone keeping an eye on the other members of the Zaleski family and had followed Eddie here? The police, perhaps? William Pinkerton might know.

If the police were indeed monitoring the Zaleskis, Miss Pelley could become entangled in a scandal that would have serious repercussions for her great-uncle. As Eddie had pointed out, there was still "bad feeling" about the unions, and unease about potential bomb plots lingered in the public mind after the Haymarket affair last May. To have a relation involved with people whom the police and newspapers considered bomb-making anarchists could not be beneficial to a legislative career.

I stood, and the young man rose politely. "Eddie, go home and wait for a message from me. Don't come back here unless I tell you so, you understand?" The last thing I needed was his presence bringing more strange men to lurk in my shrubbery.

He nodded.

The girl gave him a wan smile. "Thanks, Eddie."

After clasping her hand briefly in goodbye, he let himself out.

She helped clear the table. I rinsed the glasses, passing them to her to dry.

"What happens now?" she asked.

"We'll try to persuade your uncle to allow you and Anna to travel to Washington to stay with him. I can accompany you there to make sure you arrive safely. In the meantime"—I watched her smother a yawn—"go back to bed. I'll let you know when we have word from him."

She passed over the dishcloth. "I thought you were just a prim-and-proper spinster lady running a boardinghouse. But nothing seems to unsettle you." She looked up and met my eye. "Who are you, really? Why did Mr. Wynch bring me here?"

I draped the cloth on the drying rack and followed her out. "We'll have plenty of time to exchange our life stories on the train ride, Miss Pelley."

It took two days, a number of telegram exchanges, and even a long-distance telephone call from William Pinkerton to Senator Cullom before we finally reached an understanding.

"He's none too pleased at the prospect of not one but two young ladies showing up at his doorstep," William Pinkerton said, as we sat in his office the day before I was to leave. It was a Sunday, but we were accustomed to irregular hours at the agency. "It's a very busy time for him—something about working out a compromise on an important bill—so he is reluctant to take on new distractions. Also, his wife is traveling with their daughters. Supervision of the new arrivals will fall to the housekeeper."

"Thank heaven you were able to make him see the importance of the trip."

Pinkerton made a face. "Given Miss Pelley's involvement with the Zaleskis, I don't see that he has a choice."

"Have you been able to determine if the police are having the family watched?"

He hooked his thumbs in his vest and leaned back in his chair, as he was wont to do when hashing out a knotty problem. "There is certainly surveillance going on at the Zaleski home, and Frank has seen the same man lurking near *your* house as well, beyond the first night you detected him."

"He returned to my house?"

"Yes, on two occasions. Frank nearly caught him the last time, so we have a good description to go by. We're checking our files."

I shifted uneasily in my chair. "Why my house? Eddie hasn't been back there."

He shook his head. "I tried learning more through official channels, but the chief of police is countering my questions with several of his own, regarding my interest in the case. Naturally, I cannot violate the confidentiality of a client, so we are at a stalemate."

"Who is our client now? Surely it is no longer Miss Rotenberg."

He gave a snort. "The woman is parsimonious in the extreme. Her retainer barely covered Frank's cab fare. Cullom is our client now."

I was hoping he'd say that. Perhaps a new stove *was* in our future. "I will be compensated for my care of Claudine Pelley these past few days, as well as for accompanying both young ladies by train to Washington?"

He nodded. "You shall be *well* compensated." He passed over an envelope. "Your tickets, along with money for expenses. Cullom has even arranged sleeper accommodations for the three of you."

I tucked the envelope in my reticule. "Excellent."

CHAPTER 3

MONDAY, JANUARY 10, 1887

The porter had just taken charge of our luggage on the platform at Union Depot when I spotted Frank Wynch's tall, lean form shouldering through the crowd.

I turned to Miss Pelley, who was offering her handkerchief to Anna—the coal smoke was thick today—and gave her a nudge. "I'll be back in a moment. Wait here."

His forehead smoothed in relief when he caught sight of me. "I feared I missed you."

"The train is due any minute now. What's wrong?"

He passed me an envelope. "Information about the man who was watching your house and the Zaleskis'. Name's Leonard Crill. He's definitely not from the police, but we don't know who has hired him or why."

"Who was he watching? The Zaleskis or Miss Pelley?"

He shrugged. "Either one is a possibility. Or he could have been watching you, then followed Eddie back to his house, just to be thorough. Any recent cases where you may have made an enemy?"

I thought back. "Not that I'm aware."

"Well, I wanted you to have this before you left. I've included a complete description, the bits of his background we know, and the aliases he uses."

I caught my breath. "You believe he will follow us to Washington."

His eyes narrowed in a troubled expression. "I dearly wish I could accompany you, Pen, but Pinkerton needs me for a job. Keep your eyes open."

By the time we reached our seats and settled our belongings, the train was pulling away from the station. My young charges, heads together, fixed their gaze upon the passing landscape as the railcar picked up speed. I smiled to myself at the sight of two former farm girls gawking at the novelty of train travel. Their excitement was contagious.

Anna Zaleski, though the same age as Claudine Pelley, was taller and stockier, with pale, fluffy hair arranged in charming ringlets, a pockmarked face, and a shy smile. She was certainly the most ladylike of the two, gloved hands folded in her lap, knees together and feet on the floor, even as she leaned excitedly toward the window. Claudine, on the other hand, had tucked her feet under her in her seat and was practically kneeling upon her chair as she craned her neck for a better look.

"Miss Pelley, you may have my seat by the window, provided you keep your feet on the floor." That was the extent I was willing to go to amend her behavior. I wasn't hired to be her instructor in comportment.

With a quick glance at her friend's posture, she blushed. "Thank you."

We switched seats, she by the window across from Anna and me sitting beside her friend. I left them to their chatter and pulled out Frank's report.

Leonard Crill. Burglar, second-story man

    Aliases: "Lightfoot" Lenny, John Leonard

    Description: thirty-seven years old. Born in New York City. Moved to Chicago in 1880, after release from Sing Sing for burglary. Plumber by trade. Height, six feet, two inches. Weight, 180 pounds. Dark brown hair, brown eyes, light complexion. Dark brown beard and mustache.

    Has a cross in India ink at juncture of thumb and forefinger, right hand.

    "Lightfoot" Lenny got his name from his ability to break into houses and ransack them without waking the occupants. Has been known to imprudently leave a taunting note for his victims, which helped convict him in '75. Surprisingly agile for his size. During the '60s and early '70s, traveled up and down the East Coast in the company of the Tracey gang of burglars and sneak thieves. Participated in a number of jewelry store break-ins and second-story jobs during that time. His exploits are well-known to law enforcement in New York, Baltimore, and Richmond. Has been in and out of several penitentiaries up to 1880. Arrested only once since then. Last December in Chicago, Crill was taken into custody for a pawn shop burglary. Charges were dropped, but no information available as to why. Suspected in several recent second-story break-ins. Nothing proved.

Frank scrawled an addendum below the report: *Perhaps he has learned to stop leaving notes for his victims that could incriminate him.*

I tucked away the sheet with a sigh. A most unsavory, arrogant character, by the looks of it. What were his intentions? Who had hired him? I glanced over at my companions, chatting and sharing sweets. We should be safe from misadventure during the train trip itself. The points of ingress and egress in a railcar were constricted and observable. But meal stops and the time spent in the Pittsburgh station awaiting our connection were fraught with risk.

I unfolded the timetable. The lunch stop in Huntington was at 1:50, then the dinner stop in Marion at 7:10. Each meal break lasted twenty minutes, a frantic time when dozens of passengers simultaneously rushed to purchase and consume their food. If Lightfoot Lenny was indeed following us, it would be the perfect opportunity to strike. But was that his intent? I would have to assume so. I looked over at Miss Pelley. I would need an ally if this was to work. But was the young lady mature enough, or would she prove a hindrance?

A few hours later, Anna began to doze, and I saw my opportunity. My charge was staring idly out the window. She looked up as I sat beside her.

"Have you had a pleasant trip so far, Miss Pelley?" I asked.

She nodded. "But I'd much prefer you call me Claudine. You sound like Miss Rotenberg when you address me as 'Miss Pelley.'"

I chuckled as she pursed her mouth in a prudish imitation of the headmistress. "Very well—Claudine." I shook her hand in mock formality. "And I am Penelope. My friends call me Pen."

Her expression turned wistful. "Am *I* your friend?"

"I would like that very much." Perhaps it was a bit unusual for a chaperone to be on such informal terms with her charge, but I needed the girl to trust me. I'd already seen that the heavy-handed authoritative approach did not work with her. "I have a few questions for you, if you don't mind."

She sat up attentively. "Of course."

"During your time at the school, did you notice any strangers lurking about the grounds?"

She frowned. "What sort of strangers? You mean men? They would stand out a mile, and Rutabaga wouldn't have allowed it."

"So, no man ever tried to approach you? Perhaps on a school excursion?"

"Ah, I see your point. I do remember…yes, a couple of gentlemen tried to approach a group of us just before Christmas —we were at the art gallery—but no one spoke with me in particular. The chaperones quickly shooed them away." She nodded toward her sleeping friend. "Anna came along, too."

Nothing out of the ordinary there. I smothered a sigh. If Lightfoot Lenny wasn't following Claudine, perhaps he was following me. But for what purpose? *Any recent cases where you may have made an enemy?* Frank had asked. I closed my eyes to concentrate.

"Pen?" Claudine asked, rousing me from my thoughts. "What's wrong? Is there a man following us?"

Miss Rotenberg was right—the girl was quick-witted. There was no point in prevaricating. "I'm not sure." I recounted Frank's discoveries about the man watching our houses. Her eyes widened, but I was relieved to see that she was not given to hysterics.

"Why would he be following *me*?" she asked.

"He could be following Anna, because of the police interest in her family. But the police wouldn't hire a criminal for such a task, and it doesn't explain why he was spotted observing my boardinghouse, days after Eddie left. Anna has never been there."

"Yes, that is perplexing."

"There is another possibility, completely unrelated to you. He may have been hired by someone wanting to establish *my* movements. For what purpose, I don't know." I grimaced. If that were true, then why watch the Zaleski house?

"*Your* movements? Why would you draw such attention?" she asked.

I dropped my voice and leaned in. "You wondered why Mr. Wynch brought you to me. Well…I'm a Pinkerton, too."

Her mouth formed a silent *o*.

I gave her a moment.

"I thought there was more to you than met the eye," she said at last. "How extraordinary! I didn't know there was such a thing as lady detectives."

I gave a wry smile. "It is not common."

"So, it's possible that someone has a grudge against you from a previous…case? Have you any idea who?"

I grimaced. "Not yet. But you must keep my identity confidential. Tell no one, not even Anna."

"Of course."

"In the meantime, we should remain observant and stay together, especially when we exit the train. You and Anna mustn't wander off."

She nodded. "You can count on me."

Only two dozen of us disembarked for lunch in Huntington, so it was fairly easy to observe everyone. I saw two men who might have fit Leonard Crill's description, but one was accompanied by a lady and the other by a fellow businessman, judging by his attire. I was convinced we were looking out for a lone man. He had employed that *modus operandi* before. Human beings are creatures of habit.

Claudine was scanning the crowd as well, though much less discreetly. Her nervous back-and-forth glances drew even Anna's notice, who frowned in confusion.

I gave Claudine a nudge. "You are drawing attention to yourself," I whispered.

She glared. "I am not as practiced in the art as you," she retorted under her breath.

I shook my head. Perhaps it was a mistake to reveal as much as I had.

We got our food and ate quickly, re-boarding just in time. I wasn't sure what to conclude about Lightfoot Lenny not yet making an appearance. He might have opted to stay aboard, judging that he could not blend in with so few people about. If that was the case, the dinner stop would provide him a better opportunity.

On the other hand, he might not be on the train at all, and I was worried for nothing.

We spent a pleasant afternoon in the ladies' parlor car, which was the only interval where I felt I could draw an easy breath. No man besides the porter or conductor would dare set foot in here. Anna and Claudine shared the fashion pages from *Harper's*—I left them to debate the merits of the shortened day-train and *soutache* embellishments—while I regaled them with the occasional lovelorn letter from the local paper's agony column.

It was going on dusk when Anna got up to browse through the magazine rack for fresh material. Claudine came to sit beside me. "Do you still believe he's on the train? I didn't see anyone suspicious at the Huntington stop."

"True," I conceded. "However, if he's here, he will want to make sure of us at the dinner break in Marion. We'll keep an eye out for him there."

"How does he know we haven't gotten off at one of the other stops by now, in order to avoid him?" Claudine asked.

"But he doesn't know that we—" I broke off. I'd assumed the man wasn't aware that we knew of him. However, Frank had nearly caught Leonard Crill the last time he was watching the house. Each man had had a good look at the other. That meant Crill could have realized we were on to him when he saw Frank talking with me at the station.

The girl watched my face anxiously.

"I believe you're right, Claudine. He *would* want to make sure we had not disembarked."

"What do we do? I hate sitting around and waiting for someone else to act."

As did I. But perhaps there was a way to gain the advantage. "If I were keeping a surreptitious eye to make sure someone stayed aboard the train," I mused aloud, "I would find a vantage point where I could observe the passengers disembark at each stop." I met Claudine's eye and smiled. "You have given me an idea." I got up and smoothed my skirts. "You and Anna remain here. Promise me?"

She nodded.

"Good. I'll be back shortly."

She grinned. "I think I know what you're going to do."

I could feel my smile matching hers. "I don't doubt it." No wonder this young lady ran circles around Frank in the city. I was glad we were on the same side.

CHAPTER 4

I checked my lapel watch as I left the parlor car. Five minutes past six o'clock. According to the timetable, the train was to stop in Kenton next, at six-eleven. I had only a few minutes to find a favorable lookout point.

Watching the watcher had its risks of course, but my heart felt lighter than it had all day. Taking an active role is more suited to my nature. Far better to be the hunter than the quarry.

I opted for the open-air platform at the back of the train, only two cars behind us. However, passengers blocking the aisle to gather their belongings and porters making their way to the exits meant I could not move as quickly as I wished. The train had already pulled into the station by the time I reached the caboose. A number of quizzical looks were cast my way as I opened the back door to the viewing deck and stepped out in the chill January air. What lady voluntarily goes outside in the cold without even a shawl? Only a heedless one worried about a pursuer, it seemed.

I shivered and hugged my arms as I craned my neck around the railing for a better look along the line of cars. The station was poorly lit at the platform edge. I could only make out faces when they appeared in individual pools of light from the porters' lanterns.

My angle was an unfortunate one. The deck at the back of the train was designed for views of the sweeping vistas or quaint towns one was passing through, rather than looking forward along the railcars. I needed a better angle. After a glance around to make sure I wasn't observed, I hitched up my hem and swung a leg over the railing to straddle it. Now I was in a better position to lean away and observe the line of cars, though heaven help me if I were caught in such an unseemly posture. I smiled briefly, thinking of the Miss Rotenbergs of this world who would be scandalized by a grown woman acting in such a manner.

No heads were stuck out of windows on this side of the train. A few straggling passengers were climbing down the steps by the time I got into position, the tunic-clad porters assisting ladies with one arm and swinging suitcases out of the way with the other. From the center exit of the train, a tall man in a dark overcoat hopped down the steps, passing back a valise to a stout woman once she had gained the platform and giving her a slight bow. I stiffened. This one matched the description of Lightfoot Lenny. The height and build looked right, as did the pale complexion, reflected in the lantern light. I couldn't see the color of his eyes at this distance, but he had a full, dark beard and dark hair that touched his nape.

What on earth—? Was he getting *off* the train?

No. The porter tipped his cap to him as the man swung easily by the handrail to climb back aboard. He was merely helping the lady exit the train. It was a clever way to ensure he saw everyone who disembarked.

I must admit that, in my confusion as to his intent—I never expected such an approach—I lingered too long, perched atop the viewing platform's side railing. I didn't realize my lapse until the man caught sight of me. He froze. I quickly climbed back down and slipped inside, heart pounding. I must get to the girls. Now that Lightfoot Lenny knew he had been found out, I had no idea what he would do next.

The train was pulling away from the station and picking up speed. I passed with difficulty through the back two cars, at one point having to grab a handhold to keep from landing in a gentleman's lap as we took a curve. "I beg your pardon," I murmured, moving on. At last I reached the ladies' parlor car. To my surprise, the door was locked. I put my face to the window, peering through the gap in the curtains. Was that movement? I tapped on the glass.

A coffee-complexioned porter, rag in hand, opened it a crack. "Sorry, ma'am, the car's closed for cleanin'. We'll be open after the dinner stop in Marion."

I groped in my pocket for a coin and pressed it into his hand. "There were two young ladies in here earlier. Did you send them back to their seats?"

The man chuckled as his fingers curled around the coin. "We don' tell nobody where to go, ma'am. Folks don' like it, coming from us Georges. But I recollect the misses yer talking 'bout. Didn' want to leave, but rules is rules. If they didn' go back to their seats, mebbe they went to the other parlor car? Near the front of the train. It ain't for ladies' only, but it's nice 'nuff."

I was already hurrying down the corridor before he'd finished his sentence, scolding myself for the sick feeling of dread clutching my abdomen. *Stop it.* The man cannot get them alone, and he wouldn't dare do anything in front of other passengers. I checked for the girls as I passed our assigned seats. Empty.

I was about three railcars away from the front of the train—having just coughed and sputtered my way through the corridor adjoining the smoking car—when I encountered a tearful, shivering Claudine in the sheltered vestibule between the cars. She clutched the railing with one hand and plied her handkerchief to her eyes with the other.

"Claudine! What are you doing here? Where is Anna?" For

want of a better spot, I stepped out to join her on the lurching, swaying space, which was only partly shielded from the elements. A less than congenial place for a discussion, I can tell you.

"Anna and I argued about where to go after they closed the ladies' parlor." She sniffed. "I wanted to wait for you back at our seats, but she insisted upon a more social atmosphere. You didn't want me to tell her about Lightfoot Lenny, so I couldn't explain." She sighed. "We had a terrible quarrel, and she walked off. I was trying to collect myself before finding you." She blew her nose noisily into her kerchief.

I turned her toward the door. "I'm sure she's fine, but we should catch up to her all the same. I imagine she has gotten over her pique by now."

"Did you see him?" she asked.

"I did. Unfortunately, he observed me as well. He will be on his guard now, as must we."

The front parlor car was crowded with patrons reading, chatting, and knitting by the light of the wall sconces. We finally spotted Anna in the far corner and navigated a path around book racks, swivel chairs, skirts, and trouser legs. As we approached, I stopped short. The man I had made eye contact with was now seated beside the girl, in close conversation. I recognized the dark hair and beard, the pale face. I could also see, now, that he had an inked cross beside the thumb of his right hand. It was undoubtedly Lightfoot Lenny.

This would not do at all.

"Who are you, sir, and why are you accosting this young lady?" I asked, my tone icy. I had not troubled to keep my voice low, which caused heads to turn. Several matrons now glared at the man. *Good.*

Lightfoot Lenny, it seemed, did not rattle easily. He stood and gave a short bow. "My apologies, madam." He turned to go. As he brushed past me, he leaned over to murmur in my ear. His voice had the raspy wheeze of a long-time smoker. "See you in Washington, Miss Hamilton."

I stiffened. Once he was gone, I clutched the seat back of the chair he had just vacated and shakily lowered myself into it. Claudine pulled up another chair. "Was that him?" she whispered. "What did he say to you?" Her brows knit together.

I shook my head. "Later."

Anna watched us, her teeth tugging at her lower lip.

"Why were you conversing with a strange man, Miss Zaleski?" I kept my voice low but no less stern. "Surely you know better than that. I doubt your mother would approve."

The girl looked at her hands. "But he was so kind. He saw I was distressed. He merely wished to be of assistance. He was quite the gentleman. We got to talking about all sorts of things, and it took my mind off—" She hesitated, glancing at Claudine. "Well, I'm sure she told you already. Anyway, he was most agreeable."

"No doubt he was," I said tartly. "However, I happen to know this man's background." I leaned in. "He is a schemer and a thief. He has served time in prison."

Anna's mouth dropped open.

"You are to avoid him in the future," I went on. "You have given out too much information as it is."

"She has?" Claudine glared at her friend. "What did you say to him?"

"We only exchanged idle pleasantries," Anna said defensively.

I blew out a breath. "I do not consider sharing our destination and my name an exchange of *idle pleasantries*. Does he know Claudine's name as well?" Although, to be fair to Anna, he may have known our names already.

Anna bit her lip. "He introduced himself, so naturally I did the same—"

"What did he say his name was?" Claudine cut in.

"John Leonard."

One of the aliases on Frank's list. "Go on," I prompted. "What did you discuss?"

Anna grimaced. "I must admit, I may have let slip that we were headed for Washington..." Her voice trailed off.

I glanced at Claudine, plucking abstractedly at the folds of her skirt. "Try not to worry," I reassured her.

Claudine met my eye. "I've seen him before."

"You have? Where?"

"Remember you asked me about strange men who may have approached me, and I told you about the museum tour?"

I nodded.

"One of them was him."

So, Miss Pelley *was* the target. To what end?

I could feel the train slowing, and the conductor appeared in the doorway. "We're approaching the station in Marion, folks. Those continuing on may disembark for dinner, but twenty minutes only, please! We must keep to our timetable."

The dinner break passed without incident, though it rattled one's nerves to see Lightfoot Lenny, not troubling to conceal himself now, seated a few tables away from us, tucking into a chop and boiled potatoes.

When we returned to our car—thankfully leaving behind our shadow—the porter had already made up our beds for the night. He lingered in the car to fluff pillows, draw shades, and collect tips. I added our contribution. We took turns in the tiny washroom, tucked ourselves into our bunks, and extinguished the lights.

The few times I have traveled in a Pullman, I've had no trouble falling asleep. The rocking motion, the rhythmic clacking of the wheels upon the rails, the feeling of being cozily tucked into a well-cushioned space—the effect is soporific. Usually. Tonight was a different matter entirely. My ears attuned to every squeak, rattle, footfall, and sigh. I turned restlessly in the confined space until I was obliged to climb down and shake free my twisted nightdress. Before I hopped back in my bunk to try again to sleep —we were getting into Pittsburgh before six in the morning, and our wakeup call would be an early one—I peeked between the curtains of Claudine's and Anna's bunks. Each girl slept soundly, as only hearty youth can.

CHAPTER 5

TUESDAY, JANUARY 11, 1887

*T*he wait for our connection in Pittsburgh was long and tedious. I struggled to stay awake as we passed the time in the passenger lounge, seated among a group of chatty matrons who plied the young ladies with stick candy and a barrage of questions. Claudine and Anna countered it all with demure thanks and polite evasions, respectively.

Claudine Pelley's manners had improved considerably during our trip. I cannot say whether it was the influence of Anna's presence or Miss Rotenberg's absence—the young lady had a perverse, stubborn streak—that was responsible. At least the girls had mended their quarrel. I smiled as they leaned close for a better look at a chubby-cheeked infant sleeping in the arms of a proud new mama who sat nearby.

Claudine was not as lighthearted as she appeared, however. She stiffened and shot me an anxious look each time Lightfoot Lenny stuck his head in the lounge to be assured of our continued presence. Those occasions were frequent.

I had never found myself in such a disconcerting position. I had no recourse with the railroad authorities to have the man removed. He had not made any threatening gestures toward us and was not wanted for any crime. I'd considered trying to give him the slip, but with two young ladies in tow? Even if we were successful, we would need a place to stay and would have to re-board the train for Washington eventually. Crill was sure to be watching the station. We would be right back where we started.

No, the best course was to reach Cullom's establishment as quickly as possible. Claudine's great-uncle could then make the necessary arrangements to protect the girls. What sort of danger were they in? Crill's purpose was still unclear.

By ten thirty that morning, we boarded the Baltimore and Ohio train for Washington. This part of the journey would be shorter than the first, and we expected to arrive in Washington by nine twenty-five that evening. Crill hung back among the crowd of passengers, no doubt making sure that we were indeed board-ing. After that, he kept out of sight. I didn't know whether to be relieved or worried.

Although this leg of the journey was less than eleven hours long, it felt as if it would never end. My eyes felt gritty from the smoke and my sleepless night. I longed for a bath and a change of clothes, but it was unlikely I'd accomplish either before having to meet Senator Cullom.

It seemed that Claudine and Anna felt the strain of travel as well. The girls no longer gazed eagerly through the window at the passing sights. They rarely conversed beyond desultory small talk.

I pulled out the timetable once again. The first train leaving Washington tomorrow was 9:10 a.m., arriving in Pittsburgh at 8:21 p.m. Assuming I could make my report to Cullom as soon as we arrived tonight, I'd be free to leave his establishment first thing in the morning for the station. Two days after that, I'd be back at home, ordering a new stove. I hoped Cassie had been able to manage these past few days with only Sadie to help her.

There was no sign of Lightfoot Lenny when we disembarked, stiff-legged, at the station in Washington. I felt a prickle of unease, having gotten used to keeping track of his whereabouts as diligently as he had ours.

Claudine seemed as anxious as I. "I don't see him," she whispered.

"No matter," I answered, with more confidence than I felt. I prodded them to follow the stream of passengers to the cab stand.

After a lengthy wait—still no sign of Leonard Crill—we climbed into the next available cab and were on our way to Cullom's house on Iowa Circle.

I'd been to the city of Washington only once before, years ago, when I had helped Frank with a case. I smiled to myself in the dark. We had been newly married, in love, and delighted to discover that we worked well together. Of course, Frank took all the credit for our successes. It had been a challenge, years later, to get William Pinkerton to see that I was as skilled at detection as my husband.

"Look! Isn't it lovely?" Anna exclaimed, pointing off to the left. We had turned onto New Jersey Avenue and could see the gleaming row of electric streetlights in the distance, on Pennsylvania Avenue. The effect was indeed breathtaking.

"They have also electrified F Street and the grounds of the president's house," Claudine said. "It's very pretty."

"You have been to the city before?" I asked in surprise.

"Before Papa was to leave for California, he visited Uncle Shelby to discuss the arrangements. I came along and got to meet his second wife Julia and my cousins. They are all grown up, of course, but we had a lovely time. They gave us a tour. I saw them during the Christmas recess, too, back in Springfield."

At last, we pulled up to the three-story, brick rowhome at the left end of the circle that ringed the park beyond. Concrete balusters framed a set of stone steps that led to the front door. As the driver unloaded our luggage, I checked for a means by which a second-story man could access the windows and mansard roof. The eaves were deep enough for a handhold once one had gained the second story, but I saw no means for a man to climb up along the front of the building. I would have to check the back and side in daylight.

A brown-skinned maid clutched a hearth broom in one hand as she opened the door with the other. I introduced myself, and she bobbed a curtsy. "Yes'm, we been expecting you." She looked quite young, her crisp dark dress and starched white apron two sizes too large for her petite frame. Her eyes lit up when she caught sight of Claudine. "Miss Claudine! So nice to see you. This way." She latched the front door behind us, then headed for the front staircase, quickly shoving her brush into the umbrella stand along the way. I winced. The girl was going to catch it from the housekeeper if she left it there.

We followed her up the stairs.

"The maid seems friendly, but I'm surprised a girl her age holds such a position," I murmured to Claudine.

The girl nodded. "Hattie's younger than I am. We had a lot of fun together when I was here before." Then with a grimace, she added, "Until Mrs. Kroger caught us climbing the cherry tree in the backyard. Hattie got into a deal of trouble, more than I ever did."

I gave her a squint. "Aren't you a little too *old* for climbing trees, Miss Pelley?"

At first, a flash of sulky defiance crossed her face, until she took a second look at my teasing expression. "Well, it *is* becoming more difficult," she said with a wry smile. "I may give it up for good."

The maid flung open two consecutive doors at the end of the paneled hallway whose carpet runner was slightly crooked. "Mrs. Kroger says that the two young ladies can share this room"—she gestured toward the farthest door—"and you, Miss Hamilton, are to have this one." She pushed the door open a bit wider. The hinges squeaked.

"Thank you," I said, as the weary girls shuffled off to their room. "Where is Mrs. Kroger? Has she already retired for the evening?" I'd seen no sign of the senator, either.

The maid scowled. "She's in bed, all right, but it's 'cause this morning she wrenched her ankle something fierce. The scullery maid didn' put the bucket away proper. Mrs. K stepped right in it. Fired the girl on the spot as she was going down." She sighed. "More work for me, and we're short-staffed already."

I could believe it. Crooked rugs, squeaky hinges, cleaning tools thrust willy-nilly for others to trip over...I would be glad to return to my orderly life. "Is Senator Cullom at home? I must speak with him right away."

"Sorry, miss, he sent a message 'round, said he's working late. He's gonna speak with you and Miss Claudine tomorrow."

So much for leaving on the morning train. Well, at least I would be more presentable for my report.

The maid fidgeted. "Will that be all, miss? I still have to lock up for the night."

I nodded, and she hurried away.

The room was pleasant enough, decorated in a wallpaper pattern of climbing pink roses, the vanity stool and chair cushions covered in a complementary satin mauve tint. I was particularly drawn to the bed with its thick goose-down quilt covered in a white eyelet duvet. Neck stiff and joints protesting against two days of train travel, I nearly sank into it on the spot.

But I had a few things to take care of first. I set my case on the chair, turned down the bedside lamp, and crossed the darkened space to the window.

Not a vehicle in sight. The small park, around which the houses on Iowa Circle are clustered, was empty of people. A few gas lamps lit the entrance to the path.

Many consider Washington a restless sort of city, replete with politicians and deal-makers who carouse at all hours at high-society functions. While there are no doubt such pockets of activity, most of the town consists of families living on quiet streets and turning their locks for the night by ten o'clock. It was well after that now.

Movement along the pavement drew my eye. A uniformed policeman was walking his beat, his steps brisk on this cold night. I watched until he was out of sight of the streetlamps at the end of the curve of houses.

I was just about to withdraw when I noticed a man's tall silhouette skirt the edge of the path across the street, ducking the light of the lamps. My heart lurched. I'd gotten enough of a look to be sure it was Lightfoot Lenny. I recalled the most worrisome passage from Frank's report. *"Lightfoot" Lenny got his name from his ability to break into houses and ransack them without waking the occupants.*

I was not destined to get much sleep on this case, it seemed. With a last wistful look at the soft, inviting bed, I rummaged in my valise, pulled out and loaded my double-barreled derringer, and headed for the girls' bedroom. I prayed the lock on Cullom's front door would be sufficient to keep out a professional house burglar, but I wasn't counting on it.

CHAPTER 6

WEDNESDAY, JANUARY 12, 1887

*T*he blackness was thinning in the pre-dawn sky when I woke from my stiffened position in an upholstered chair. I stood and stretched. The young ladies were fast asleep. Even though my weapon stayed out of sight in my skirt pocket, the explanation for my presence had made it difficult for them to settle down. They looked angelic now, frown lines smoothed, soft hair a-tumble upon their pillows.

I pulled the chair away from where I had it blocking the door and squinted at my watch. Mercy, nearly five o'clock. Time for a short nap, followed by quick morning ablutions and a change of clothes. I'd been in the same rumpled skirt and shirtwaist since Pittsburgh. But first, I wanted to check the locks on the first floor, in case there were signs that Lightfoot Lenny had tried to break in.

I crept, shoeless and soft-footed, down the stairs. All was quiet. The staff—what was left of it—was sure to be up soon. I entered the dim foyer and inspected the front door first. It looked perfectly intact, but perhaps I should turn on the light and examine it more closely. As I reached for the lamp chain, I caught sight of the hearth broom still stuck in the umbrella stand. Hattie had indeed forgotten all about it. I pulled it out. I would leave it beside the fireplace in my room for the maid to retrieve later.

The sound of the front door latch jiggling froze me in my tracks. Why would Lightfoot Lenny wait until *now*, when it was nearly daylight, to break in? My mouth went dry. Completely forgetting about the derringer still in my pocket—some detective I was turning out to be—I raised the absurd little broom that was still in my hand, ready to strike...

And promptly whacked the middle-aged gentleman coming through the door. Dark ash scattered across his thinning pate.

He put up an arm, too late, in self-defense. "Have you lost your mind?" he barked, fumbling for the hall lamp and switching it on. He paused for breath and swept me in a glare. "Who the devil are you?" The voice was gruff, laced with annoyance and fatigue.

I could only imagine the inauspicious sight I presented, clad in creased, days-old clothing and my hair slipping from its pins. Add to that the absurdity of attacking my client with his own hearth brush, and I could kiss goodbye any favorable first impression. I felt the headache bloom behind my eyes. It was a blessing that I *had* forgotten about my derringer. The man might well be sporting a bullet hole in his once-spotless wool coat instead of the ash he was indignantly brushing off.

I drew myself up to my full height—which meant I easily met his eye—and collected what shreds of dignity I had left. "Good morning, Senator. I am Penelope Hamilton, th-the"—I cleared my throat—"the Pinkerton agent who escorted your grandniece and her companion here from Chicago."

Employing the old adage that the better part of valor is discretion, and considering that Cullom had had an all-night meeting and was as exhausted as I, we agreed to postpone an in-depth discussion until we each had a chance to rest and freshen up.

It was mid-morning by the time I came back downstairs. The girls were reading in the library, and Claudine looked up eagerly when I stuck my head in. "Uncle Shelby is waiting for you in his study."

I stiffened. "What else did he say?" I hoped he hadn't mentioned this morning's unfortunate encounter.

Anna piped up. "Just the usual pleasantries. He wanted to see if we needed anything. Such a nice gentleman."

I grimaced. As Anna had considered Lightfoot Lenny a "nice gentleman," her endorsement carried little weight.

Claudine nodded. "He did chastise me for running away from school, but he didn't seem all that angry. I could see him trying not to smile when I was telling him what it was like at that stuffy old place."

"Consider yourself lucky," I said, hoping I would be equally fortunate. "Did you tell him about the man on the train?"

Claudine crinkled her forehead. "I decided to leave that to you."

Cullom's study was the masculine space one might expect, with its deep leather chairs, oak paneling, and lingering scent of cigars. I noted, however, insinuations of a woman's touch in the silk flower arrangement atop a filing cabinet and soft gold draperies over the French doors.

He looked better rested now, the shadows beneath his deepset, gray eyes less pronounced. He had the high, domed forehead of a scholar but the prominent nose and well-defined jaw—bewhiskered as it was—of a man who knows his own mind.

He waved me toward a chair and began to pace the room. The similarity to his grandniece was striking in that moment. Each possessed a restless energy when confronted with a problem.

After an interval, I spoke. "I want to apologize again, sir, for the confusion in the front hall this morning. I hope I did not injure you?"

He gave a snort. "Hardly, though the same cannot be said for my coat. But what's done is done." He stopped pacing and fixed me with a stern eye. "Do you make it a habit to pounce upon people unawares? Pinkerton could have warned me."

I took a breath and firmly suppressed the urge to giggle. "I can explain."

"I'm listening."

"We have learned that a man named Leonard Crill"—I withdrew Frank's report from my skirt pocket and passed it over —"has been monitoring Claudine for a period of time. We do not know what object he hopes to gain by doing so. Whatever the reason, we believe he was hired by someone else, a person as yet unknown."

Cullom didn't answer as he read through the report. Finally, he looked up. "A rather disagreeable character. How long has this been going on?"

"According to your grandniece, she first noticed him before the Christmas holiday, while on a school excursion to a museum. The operative who compiled this report observed him watching Anna Zaleski's house as well as mine the last two days before we left. The man then followed us here by train from Chicago. And just last night I saw him lurking in the park across the street." I recounted the subsequent precautions I had taken to keep the girls safe.

He nodded. "When I saw you this morning, you thought I was this man—Lightfoot Lenny—coming through the door?"

I grimaced. "I was checking the lock before retiring. I'd assumed you had already returned home."

He passed a hand over his scalp and winced. "It was a long, contentious meeting. Congressmen Orrington and Rodgers... bringing up the same objections, over and over again." He half-muttered to himself, "Of course they are in Huntington's pocket, so it's no great surprise."

I recognized only one of the names. "Huntington? As in Collis P. Huntington, the railroad magnate?"

Cullom grunted. "The same. Railroad men like Huntington are fighting us tooth and nail on a piece of commercial regulation we've been trying to pass. It is the first comprehensive bill of its kind and sorely needed." He tapped the paper. "May I keep this? I'll send a message to the district captain and ask for an additional man to patrol the block at night. If we can catch this fellow, the police may be able to get the story out of him."

"You know of no reason why Lightfoot Lenny would be following Claudine?"

He frowned. "Claudine? No, none."

"What kind of staff do you have?" I asked. "Any sturdy fellows who can keep watch inside the house at night? Your locks look to be adequate, but Crill is reputed to be an accomplished second-story man."

"I have no male employees. Town living doesn't really require it. We hire the conveyances we need, and I have no need of a valet. The house itself is leased. We are not here year-round."

"Who among your staff lives in? I met the maid, Hattie, and I understand the housekeeper lives here as well. Anyone else? The cook, perhaps?"

"No, she and her daughter leave after dinner is cleaned up. There is another maid who lives with us, but she is accompanying my wife and daughters on their trip to Charlottesville. The scullery maid also lived in"—he grimaced—"but of course, she was dismissed when Mrs. Kroger was injured by her carelessness." He sighed. "I've been much too busy to see about hiring another. We shall have to make do."

I pitied Hattie's workload in the meantime. Now I could see why Cullom was not eager to have the girls come. And with the housekeeper confined to her bed, the problem was compounded: how were Claudine and Anna to be properly looked after?

"When do your wife and daughters return?" I asked.

"Not for several weeks."

"Can your wife not shorten her trip?"

He shook his head. "Her sister just had her first child. I would incur no end of righteous female indignation for even suggesting it."

"Could you send Claudine and Anna to join them there?"

He raised an eyebrow. "You propose we add two uninvited guests to a new mother's household. You recall what I said about righteous female indignation? That would be far worse."

I smiled. "Perhaps so."

"I am a simple man, Miss Hamilton." He sat back and laced his fingers over his stomach. "I only require a warm fire, a good meal, and domestic tranquility." He added, under his breath, "And a common-sense bill passed in Congress every once in a while."

"What are your future plans for Claudine? She said she only saw you briefly today and had not discussed anything long-term."

"My wife Julia will deal with the issue of Claudine's education, after she returns. She was the one who had made the arrangements with Miss Rotenberg."

I hoped Mrs. Cullom would make a better choice for Claudine's schooling this time around. It was not my concern, of course. I was only responsible for the girl's present well-being, which I wanted to be assured of before I left. "You are permitting your grandniece and her friend to stay here until your wife returns, then?"

"I don't see any other options."

"What of Miss Zaleski? How will she get home?"

"We will make sure the girl is returned safely. Julia doesn't like to leave our Springfield house closed up for long, and Chicago is *en route*. She can accompany the girl when the time comes." He frowned. "The immediate problem is supervision until my wife's return. Mrs. Kroger is now in no condition to serve in that capacity."

"There is no other female relation who could act as chaperone?"

He shook his head. "And that doesn't solve the problem of this man—Crill. The police cannot keep a constant watch upon the house."

"That's true," I conceded. "Perhaps you can hire someone local for additional surveillance. I'm sure Mr. Pinkerton could provide a recommendation."

He stayed silent, his eyes narrowing as I stood to take my leave.

It was then that I realized what he had in mind.

He reached for the bell pull. "He already has, Miss Hamilton, and I concur. *You* are to look after the young ladies and keep them safe."

I should have packed more clothing.

I took a breath, firmly pushing aside my worries for Cassie and the stove-less household I had left behind. "Of course, sir, although I wish I'd anticipated a longer visit. I'm afraid I haven't sufficient—" I broke off as Hattie stepped in the room, this time clutching a dust rag. I wondered if the girl was even conscious of the fact that she carried her cleaning tools with her wherever she went.

"You rang, sir?" she asked politely.

"Fetch Miss Pelley and Miss Zaleski, if you please."

She gave a quick curtsy and left.

Cullom smiled in my direction. "Now, then, Miss Hamilton, I am delighted you can stay. Despite your mistaken assault upon me this morning"—his lips twitched—"or perhaps because of it, I deem you a capable young woman. Pinkerton had said much the same about your qualifications when we made your original travel arrangements."

I felt my face flush at the compliment as I resumed my seat.

"Although I hope, in the future, you protect your charges with something more formidable than a hearth broom," he went on. He gave me a sharp, assessing glance. "You are armed, I trust?"

I sat back in astonishment. Never before had a client, male or female, treated me as a professional from the outset. That sort of respect had always been hard won, by the end of a case. And not always then. "Yes. A double-barreled Remington."

He winced. "Not much accuracy or firepower. Let us hope you do not need it."

"It suits my purposes, as it is more easily concealed," I said. "I can hardly walk around with a holstered Colt .45 strapped over my skirts."

He chuckled. "True enough."

Claudine and Anna appeared in the study doorway, and Cullom waved them in. "Take a seat, ladies."

As they settled themselves, he paced from window to hearth, talking over his shoulder. "Miss Hamilton has agreed to stay on as chaperone for the next few weeks, until Mrs. Cullom and my daughters return home from their trip. At some point afterward, Claudine, we will settle what school you will attend and return your friend to her home." He turned and looked at Anna. "Miss Zaleski, we will communicate with your family to ensure they agree to the plan."

Anna nodded, blonde ringlets bobbing. "What about that— man? The one on the train. Miss Hamilton said he was across the street watching the house last night."

"We are making arrangements for your safety, do not worry," Cullom said. "But you must follow our instructions fully, do you understand?" He turned to Claudine. "And you as well, my good miss. I know your headstrong ways." His look softened. "How would I explain it to your father if something happened to you while you were in my charge?"

Claudine sat up straight. "I will do as you say, Uncle Shelby. I promise."

"And you must be of aid to the staff however you can," he went on. "Make your own beds, clean up after yourselves, pick up a broom when needed. Poor Hattie will be running ragged."

"I'm no stranger to housework, Mr. Cullom," Anna said, meeting his eye.

"Neither am I," Claudine chimed in. "At the academy, we had all sorts of chores. Don't worry, Uncle—we are not ladies of leisure. I promise we won't be a burden to you."

Cullom smiled and rested a hand briefly on Claudine's shoulder. "You're a good girl. I promise it won't all be drudgery. In fact, I've been invited to an art reception and auction on Sunday evening, if you ladies wish to accompany me. You and Anna and Miss Hamilton can go shopping for pretty gowns tomorrow. Miss Hamilton will need to add to her wardrobe, anyway, now that she is staying." He smiled at me. "You may use my account at R.H. Taylor's to buy whatever you need."

"I appreciate your generosity, sir," I said, "but are you sure an excursion at this time is prudent?"

"You will be accompanied by a driver I have in mind, a good, reliable man I've used for the last few months. I'll make the necessary arrangements. Now, if you ladies will excuse me, I have a number of messages to send out."

Claudine gave her uncle a hug before she left. "Thank you," she whispered.

Cullom awkwardly returned the embrace and cleared his throat. "Go on with you, now. Try to stay out of trouble."

Before I followed the girls out, I asked, "May I send a telegram? I want to let my housemate, Cassie Leigh, know of the change in plans."

He passed over a small notepad and pencil. "Put down what you want to send, and I'll make sure it goes out."

CHAPTER 7

FRIDAY, JANUARY 14, 1887

*I*t was actually another day and a half before the arrangements were in place for our shopping excursion. There had been no sign of Lightfoot Lenny in the interim. No doubt he was keeping his distance, now that the police had increased their patrols past Cullom's house.

The young ladies were beside themselves with excitement at the prospect of having an outing at last. I, on the other hand, was trying to ignore the lump of dread in my abdomen as I pulled on my gloves and waited for the carriage to arrive.

"Would your uncle approve the purchase of a hat as well as a gown, do you think?" Anna asked, self-consciously adjusting her battered ivory straw. "I don't wish to take advantage of his generosity."

Claudine slid her hand into the crook of her friend's arm. "You shall have a new hat. I insist." She pointed. "Look! There's the carriage now."

A compact, wiry limbed man in his mid-twenties swept his cap from his head and plucked a toothpick out of his mouth when I opened the door. "Jack Porter, at yer service." He had red, kinky hair and sharp gray eyes that missed little as he looked me up and down. "You'd be Miss Hamilton, I 'spect?"

I inclined my head in acknowledgment. "The senator has apprised you of our...situation?"

"No worries, miss." He lowered his voice. "I been told what he looks like. No sign o' any such character when I pulled up, but I got a cudgel under my seat, just in case—" He broke off and bowed to the girls as they approached. "I un'erstand we are doing a bit o' shopping, ladies?" He raised his voice to a jovial tone.

"Yes, indeed," Claudine said with enthusiasm.

"Well, then, I'm your man. Jack's the name. Right this way." He popped the toothpick back into his mouth and handed us into what appeared a respectable-enough coach, though the left fender was scraped with white paint and the interior smelled a bit musty.

The mid-January morning was sunny and mild—an occasional phenomenon of Washington winters, according to Jack—so the trip was a pleasant one as we headed for the shopping district.

I spent most of the interval looking through the rear window, watching for any conveyances that might be following. In addition to horse-drawn traffic, bicyclists and pedestrians crisscrossed the streets with abandon. I saw no one suspicious.

In just a short time, we pulled up to the brick storefront of R.H. Taylor's.

Jack hopped down. "I'll wait here for you, ladies."

"We may be a while," I warned, knowing that the girls would not be denied their adventure. I needed a number of items myself.

He grinned. "I never met a lady who *didn't* take a long time shopping."

As expected, it was several hours later before we were done. We clutched as many boxes as we could carry, with the help of two clerks whom the effusive head of the women's department had pressed into service. And little wonder. The man's sales quota for the month was assured.

Anna smothered a laugh behind her brand-new kid gloves as Jack stowed our packages. "Did you see all the help we were getting? I thought the sales clerks were going to buy us lunch next!"

"Well, at least that's done," I said, "although it's a nuisance to have to return for a final gown fitting." The combination of my height and lean frame always made it difficult to find clothing that fit me properly. I felt uneasy about leaving the house again for a lengthy interval, despite Cullom's precautions. But the store's seamstress promised all would be ready for me by tomorrow afternoon. One quick try-on, and I should be done.

"Speaking of lunch," Claudine said, "I'm famished. Can we stop on the way?"

I frowned. "Perhaps we should eat at home."

"I already told Cook not to prepare lunch for us," Claudine said. "I didn't want to give her more work."

Her point was valid. I turned to Jack. "Do you know of a ladies' tearoom nearby?"

He scratched his head beneath his cap for a moment, then said, "There's Rosine's, just a few blocks down. Light fare. Soup, sandwiches, tea, cakes, and suchlike."

Claudine and Anna perked up at the mention of *cakes*.

I chuckled. "That will suffice."

As we stepped into Rosine's, my mouth watered at the aromas of simmering onion soup and yeast rolls fresh from the oven. The familiar, uneasy tightening of my abdomen returned, however, when my gaze swept over the room. Every table was occupied, as were the stools at the long lunch counter. Patrons spilled into the vestibule. If Crill had managed to follow us unnoticed, there would be no spotting him here. But the crowded environment had the advantage of imposing restraint upon the man, should he plan violence.

I frowned. It always came back to that. What was his intent? Who had hired him?

A table finally became available, and we followed the proprietress, threading our way past leather banquettes and tables laid with ivory linen, flower arrangements in milk-glass vases, and sturdy chinaware. I dodged just in time as a tall, lean, exquisitely attired gentleman stepped back to pull out a lady's chair.

"I beg your pardon!" the man exclaimed.

I caught my breath. I knew this man—the dark pencil mustache, black wavy hair, keen eyes, and wide smile. "Mr. Kendall?"

His grin deepened. "Miss Hamilton! Delightful to see you again. What brings you to Washington?"

"I could ask the same of you." My glance swept to his companion. Though a bit past her prime, she was an attractive, bejeweled woman of above-average figure and below-average manners, if one was to judge by her bold, assessing gaze. I wondered what Kendall was up to. Was he truly the reformed soul he had proclaimed when we had parted in the summer? The impeccable camel-hair jacket that fit smoothly along his trim torso was undeniably custom-tailored, and likely cost more than a month's worth of our groceries back home.

"Ah, where are my manners?" he said. "May I present my friend, Mrs. Lydia Engels. Lydia, this is Miss Penelope Hamilton."

Mrs. Engels was still seated in the chair that Kendall grasped. She stood and gave a brief nod as she collected her reticule. "We should be going, Phillip," she snapped, eyes narrowing at me in suspicion.

"Just a moment." He turned to Claudine and Anna, who tried—unsuccessfully—not to gawk at the dashing gentleman. "Aren't you going to introduce me to these charming young ladies?"

Claudine blushed to the roots of her dark hair.

How Senator Cullom would react to my introducing his grandniece to a jewel thief I did not wish to contemplate. I could only hope he would not learn of it. I kept the pleasantries short as I carried out the introductions, ending with, "Regrettably, Mr. Kendall, we must proceed to our table. We are blocking the aisle. But it was pleasant to see you again."

He pulled out a card and pressed it into my gloved hand. "Should you be in need of anything while you are in town, I'm staying at the National Hotel, not far from here. Feel free to contact me."

His lady companion sniffed and turned away. I suppressed a smile. Kendall had some fence-mending ahead of him. "Thank you."

As soon as we were seated at our table and had placed our orders, the girls launched a barrage of questions. "Who is he?" "Is he married?" "Where did you meet?"

I stuck to the truth as best as I could and avoided the temptation to embellish. That is inevitably what gets one caught out in a lie, I've learned. "I was on holiday in the Adirondacks last summer. He was staying at the same lodge. I don't know much about him, really." All too true—it's not as if the man had shared his life story with me.

We pulled out our napkins to make way for the soup course.

Anna raised a pale eyebrow. "You must know *something* about him," she said, after the server had left.

Claudine nodded. "Yes, I imagine you can tell us more than that, Miss Hamilton." She leaned forward and met my eye with an equally skeptical look that seemed to say, *You are a detective, after all.*

Drat the girl, she already knew me too well.

"Mr. Kendall said at the time that he was in the shipping business," I said. "I don't know if that is still the case. We have not corresponded. As far as his marital state, he behaves as if he is a bachelor, but of course that is no way to tell. I'm sure you are aware that such a pretense is common." I did not believe him to be married, however, remembering his words regarding a certain opera singer of which he was fond: *I couldn't possibly marry. It would not be amenable to my line of work and hardly fair to the young lady.*

The girls sighed and turned their attention to the soup.

The rest of the meal passed without incident. I was beginning to feel hopeful that Lightfoot Lenny had been deterred by Cullom's precautions. Finally, we stepped out of the restaurant and into the bright sunshine. I shaded my eyes against the glare, looking for our vehicle. It wasn't where we left it. Then, at the end of the block, I caught sight of Jack and waved. He hastily wadded up a piece of wax paper, brushed himself off, and brought the vehicle around.

"Sorry, miss. I didn't want to block traffic."

I nodded. "You saw nothing unusual?"

He shook his head.

As we pulled up to Cullom's house, however, we were in for a surprise. Coming out to greet us was a short, stocky couple of middling age, the pepper-gray-haired man in a butler's uniform and the woman dressed primly in a white shirtwaist and skirt of sober blue pinstripes. With a perfunctory bow in our direction, the man went over to help the driver unload our packages while the woman approached us.

"I am Mrs. Webb. Senator Cullom has hired me and my husband"—she nodded toward the man—"to fill in as housekeeper and butler, until Mrs. Kroger has recovered. A few maids have been taken on as well." She frowned. "The house has been sadly neglected, with only the young Negro girl to tend to it."

"Hattie," I said. "Her name is Hattie. She works very hard."

The woman waved a hand. "Yes, yes. I'm sure she tried."

"Your presence is certainly a surprise, Mrs. Webb. The senator never mentioned any plans to hire more staff."

Mrs. Webb shrugged. "I wasn't privy to his reasons. The agency contacted us that we were needed, and here we are." She looked up at me, eyes narrowing intently. "You look tired, Miss—

Hamilton, isn't it? I can have a warm bath drawn for you, if you'd like."

"Perhaps later."

With a nod, she turned away.

Jack was about to step back into the carriage to leave when I approached him. "Can you do me a favor?" I murmured. I fished in my reticule for pencil and pad and scribbled a quick note for Senator Cullom: *Did you hire the Webbs?*

His eyes narrowed as I passed it over for him to read. He jerked a thumb toward the butler and his wife as they followed the young ladies into the house. "You don't think he hired 'em?" He kept his voice low.

"Let us say I'd prefer to err on the side of caution. Can you give him this and bring back his reply? If you can find him." I hoped Cullom was not sequestered in some committee meeting.

He grinned and tipped his cap. "Well, now, yer a right unusual lady. Don't worry, miss. I'll find 'im."

By the time Jack returned, I had at least assured myself that the Webbs were adept at their duties. The floors were swept, the furniture dusted, hinges were oiled, and fires burned brightly in the parlor, library, and bedroom hearths. Not a broom or rag in sight. The Cullom home had become much more comfortable in a short span of time.

The bed linens had been changed as well. I checked the hiding place in my bedroom for my lockpicks and logbook, behind the bottom dresser drawer. The nearly invisible blonde hairs were still in place across the top of the pouch, undisturbed. Good.

I ran outside as soon as I heard Jack's carriage pull up to the curb. He leaned out. "All's well, miss. Mr. Cullom says he hired 'em yesterday but forgot to tell you."

I blew out a breath. "Thank you, Jack. Anything else? Did he say when he was returning tonight?"

"He'll be home for supper and says he's bringing comp'ny." He jerked a thumb toward the house. "Says the Webbs already know 'bout it."

"Company? Do you know who?"

He shook his head, then looked past me. I turned and saw the butler was standing on the stoop, eyeing Jack.

"I'd best be off now," Jack said.

"Thank you," I said.

Webb opened the door for me. "What'd the driver come back for? You two had a prolonged conversation."

What a nosy man. My mother would never have stood for such behavior in our butler when I was a child. Of course, neither my mother nor I was mistress of the Cullom household. I was hired help, on the same footing as Webb. "Jack was merely returning my…my handkerchief." I groped in my pocket and held one up. It wouldn't do for Webb to know I had inquired about him and his wife. "I must have dropped it in the conveyance without realizing it."

He bowed deferentially, his face now smoothed and expressionless. "Quite conscientious of him."

"Indeed." It was on the tip of my tongue to ask about our dinner guests, but I stopped myself just in time. I shouldn't possess that bit of information. Webb might make the connection to my interchange with the driver and thence back to Cullom. I don't know why, but I still felt on my guard around those two. The departure of Lightfoot Lenny—if truly a departure it was—and the arrival of new staff…well, I don't like coincidences. Perhaps a chat with the original housekeeper, Mrs. Kroger, was in order.

I found her in the kitchen, nursing a grudge along with her injured ankle. She sat in a rocking chair positioned in view of the door to the dining room, her wrapped foot propped on a stool, crutches within easy reach. "Be careful with the good china," she barked to a red-headed maid I didn't recognize. "It's Wedgewood.

Carry only one piece at a time." The girl bobbed and hugged the platter to her bosom.

"You seem to be feeling better, Mrs. Kroger," I said.

She turned to me with snapping dark eyes. "It doesn't matter whether I'm better or not, Miss Hamilton. I cannot sit idly by while the household is being upended. That Mrs. Webb breezes in here like she owns the place, proceeds to have it scoured top to bottom as if we're contaminated with the plague! I expect nothing will be put back where it belongs."

"Do you know anything about the Webbs? Where they come from?"

"One of the agencies sent them over. That's all I know." She looked me up and down. "Is there something you need?"

I pulled down a glass from the shelf. "I'm here for some milk." I got the bottle from the ice box and remarked casually over my shoulder, "Are we having company? You mentioned the good china."

She grunted. "Two of those railroad men and their wives."

"I'm surprised Mr. Cullom would hold such an affair without his wife present."

She shrugged. "He usually doesn't, but politics makes strange bedfellows, as they say. No doubt that applies to meals as well."

The next few hours produced a flurry of preparations upstairs as well as down, as Claudine and Anna opened boxes, shook out new articles of clothing, unpinned sales tags, and debated what to wear. They were in their element, of course, even chiming in with advice for me.

"Ooh, Miss Hamilton, the burgundy tea gown you got today would be perfect for the occasion," Anna said breathlessly, as she held up her own prospect in front of the looking glass, "It is quite becoming on you."

I grimaced. "Let us hope it wasn't horribly wrinkled in transit. I had better see to it."

I was nearly ready when Hattie knocked. "Telegrams for you, miss," she called through the door.

"It's all right, Hattie. Come in."

She watched as I opened them. The first was from William Pinkerton.

SENATOR C. ALREADY SENT YOUR RETAINER, VERY GENEROUS AMT. QUES: IS LC STILL THERE? NO SIGN OF HIS RETURN. ZALESKI BROTHER NOW IN CUSTODY.

I re-read it. I couldn't tell Pinkerton much about Leonard Crill, but I would send him a response nonetheless. I was more troubled by the thought of Eddie Zaleski sitting in jail. Poor Anna. How was I to tell her?

The next was from Cassie.

ALL IS WELL. PINKERTON SENT FUNDS FROM YOUR ACCOUNT. WILL ORDER STOVE TOMORROW. ~C.

I breathed an easy sigh. At least I didn't have to worry about the state of affairs back home.

Hattie's soft voice broke into my thoughts. "Miss, is there an answer?"

"Yes, to one of them. Just a moment." I scribbled a quick reply to Pinkerton and placed it into her hands. "Thank you, dear. Are you having an easier time of it, now that you have more help?"

She shrugged. "Easier in some ways, harder'n others. The Webbs are a bossy lot."

I nodded. "At least it's only temporary."

She frowned. "I dunno 'bout that, miss. Mrs. Kroger got a telegram, too. Her sister in Boston needs her. Family emergency."

"Did she say what the emergency was?"

Hattie shook her head. "But she's taking the train up there tomorrow. How she's gonna get by on a sprained ankle, I can't even think."

"Well," I said with a smile, "if anyone can manage it, Mrs. Kroger can."

CHAPTER 8

$\mathcal{I}$ headed downstairs, the girls promising to follow me in a short while. As I passed the kitchen, Webb hurried by with a tray of highball glasses and unidentifiable hors d'oeuvres.

"Where is everyone?" I asked.

He tipped his head towards the parlor. "The ladies are settled in there, while the senator, Mr. Huntington, and Mr. Graham are in the study." He turned away with a distracted air. "Excuse me, miss."

I couldn't help but sympathize. The new staff had barely gotten settled before having to orchestrate a dinner affair.

I hesitated in the corridor. Should I wait for Claudine and Anna before heading to the parlor? It would spare me the sole burden of tedious conversation with the matrons. I lingered near Cullom's study, staying in sight of the main stairs. Webb was coming out already, holding the empty tray at his side and pulling the door shut to muffle the sound of a raised voice. At least one in their group was agitated.

Naturally, I had to find out why. As soon as Webb was out of view, I went over and put my ear to the door.

A man—elderly, I suspected, as his voice held a bit of a quaver

—was saying, "…not enough time for us to respond, to propose alternatives—"

Cullom cut him off, his voice tinged with impatience. "Come, now. What you truly object to is not being able to continue your abuses with impunity. You have had any number of chances to respond. Our committee traveled extensively just to speak with you fellows about the measures in the bill, even reviewing the wording, line by line, with Fink and Blanchard in New York."

"He has a point, sir." It was the voice of a younger man.

"None of you took us seriously," Cullom said. "You said I risked my reputation taking on such a cause. But your attitude has changed, now that it is on the verge of passing."

"Do not be so sure of that," the elderly man snarled. "I have powerful allies in both the House and Senate, and a few other tricks up my sleeve."

"What is that supposed to mean?" Cullom's voice was sharp with suspicion.

"Now, now," the younger man soothed, a trace of laughter in his voice, "we have come here to relax and share the senator's hospitality, Collis. He has been trying to work with us all the while, and you must admit that his version is at least better than Reagan's."

"Pen," Claudine's voice whispered.

I stifled an exclamation, straightening up to see Claudine and Anna grinning at having caught me *in flagrante*. I needed to work on dividing my attention. Thank heaven it hadn't been Webb.

I ushered them toward the parlor. "All right, you two. Stop smirking. I was simply curious."

"Anything interesting?" Claudine asked, eyes still gleaming with merriment.

"Sadly, no. Legislation talk." I prodded them through the parlor door.

Claudine nodded. "The Interstate Commerce Act. Uncle talked of little else over the Christmas holiday. It drove Aunt Julia to distraction, I can tell you," she added, dropping her voice to a murmur as two women in their middle thirties looked up in curiosity.

Claudine, to my astonishment, gave a dainty, ladylike curtsy. "Thank you for coming to visit us here at my great-uncle's house. I am Miss Claudine Pelley. This is my friend, Miss Anna Zaleski, and this is Miss Penelope Hamilton, an acquaintance who accompanied us on our trip from Chicago."

I noticed that Claudine had stated only the bald facts, leaving the women to draw their own conclusions about my status in the household.

"Is there anything you require?" Claudine went on. "I believe dinner will be served shortly."

I exchanged a glance with Anna, who looked as bemused as I. At least some of Miss Rotenberg's training at the ladies' academy seemed to have taken root.

The lady sitting farthest from the fire—it *was* a bit warm in here—turned out to be Huntington's wife, Arabella, whose broad forehead, soft, rounded cheeks, and rosebud lips gave her a Victorian, candy-box prettiness. She inclined her dark head and gestured for Claudine to take the chair beside her. "We are perfectly comfortable, thank you. It is a pleasure to meet you, dear."

"We understand that Mrs. Cullom and her daughters are out of town at the moment," added the other lady, Mrs. Beatrice Graham. She was a buxom woman with bright eyes and an animated countenance. Her rigid torso suggested an exceptionally tight corset, but she made up for her immobility with wide hand gestures that took in the entire room. "You are doing a splendid job as hostess in her absence, I must say."

Claudine blushed. "Thank you, Mrs. Graham."

Webb stepped into the parlor, the gentlemen standing behind him. "Dinner is served, ladies," he intoned.

Introductions were made as the gentlemen helped seat us

around the dining table, laid with gilt-edged, snowy linen and a polished brass candelabra at the center that gleamed by the light of ivory beeswax candles. I'd already surmised, based upon who took whose arm on our way to the dining room, that the elderly gentleman with the white push-broom mustache, neatly trimmed beard, Roman nose, and glowering expression was Collis P. Huntington.

The other gentleman, Jacob Graham, was a good bit younger than Huntington. He was in his early fifties by my guess, though his vigorous air gave the impression of someone even younger. He walked with a little lift to his stride, as if he were springing on his toes.

Claudine decided to lead the conversation as the soup was served. The young lady was certainly taking her hostess duties seriously. "Mr. Huntington, I understand you build railroad lines. That sounds quite gratifying, to help connect the people of our country and enable them to move about."

Huntington's gruff look softened. "There are certainly bright spots to my work, young lady." He glanced at Cullom. "Although it has been exasperating of late."

When Cullom didn't trouble to answer, Huntington went on. "It is not only people, Miss Pelley, but goods that are moved about." He gestured to the plate of crudités at her elbow. "I would be willing to wager that the celery resting there comes from the farms of Michigan and the coal heating the oven that baked this"—he tapped the roll in his napkin—"comes from a West Virginia mine."

Cullom nodded. "Quite so."

"How interesting!" Anna exclaimed. "I had not considered it before."

Jacob Graham leaned forward eagerly. "Railroads are the beating heart of America. Had it been hemmed in and burdened in its early days by spurious government regulation, we would not be the industrial power we are today or enjoy the comforts we have come to expect." He studiously avoided looking at Cullom, but it was obvious to whom the speech was directed.

"I confess, Mr. Graham, I don't know what you do," I said, sitting back so the footman could remove my bowl. "Are you in the railroad business as well?"

He smiled. "Not exactly. Collis and I have worked together on a few projects, but the details are too tedious for a lady's ears. I am in the shipbuilding and transportation line, though nothing near as extensive—" He broke off as the salmon was served.

"I have brought your favorite plum sauce to enjoy with the fish, sir," Webb said, placing a small saucer in front of him.

Graham's expression brightened. "Ah, thank you." Webb bowed and headed back to the kitchen.

Huntington watched the butler leave. "The man is a treasure. Always solicitous of one's preferences." He glanced at Graham. "He must have remembered your fondness for the stuff the times you dined with us."

Mrs. Graham chuckled. "I believe Jacob dines with you more often than he does at home."

Graham smiled at his wife. "We've had a great deal to keep us occupied lately."

"I'm obliged for the referral," Cullom said, nodding toward Huntington. "Webb and his wife are working out quite well."

"A funny little fellow," Huntington said. "Used to be a painter, shared a studio with other artists over at the Corcoran Gallery. Turned to butler service when he couldn't sell his work."

"I've seen his work," Arabella Huntington interjected. "He's a far better butler, believe me."

"Why did you let him go?" I asked.

"He left us, actually, desiring a longer-term position that would also employ his wife," Huntington said. "We already have a housekeeper and are in town for only a few months."

Mrs. Huntington nodded. "We plan to head back to New York this week, in fact."

Huntington cleared his throat. "That has not yet been decided, Bella."

After an awkward pause, the conversation shifted to topics that Graham would undoubtedly consider congenial to "a lady's ear"—the weather, the dreadful state of traffic in the downtown shopping district, and the upcoming art auction.

"I am most anxious to acquire a particular piece at the auction." Beatrice Graham set down her water glass and turned to her husband. "You remember the Siebert watercolor I told you about?"

Graham's mouth twitched. "Not precisely, my dear. We talk of so many things."

"A Siebert watercolor?" Arabella Huntington queried, eyes narrowed. "Surely you do not mean *The Heartbreak of Iolanthe?*"

Mrs. Graham nodded. "The very same. The colors will go splendidly in my morning room."

"But that is the piece *I* intend to purchase, as a wedding gift to my niece. She adores his watercolors."

"Not if *I* have anything to say about it," Mrs. Graham retorted.

Cullom stiffened, with the guarded expression one might wear if a live snake had slithered into the room. Given his earlier comments about "female indignation," perhaps each was equally to be avoided in that man's eyes.

"Well now," he said finally, "it is high time we gentlemen excuse ourselves." He rang the bell beside his plate. "Ah, Webb—lay out the port in the study, would you?"

We ladies adjourned to the library, where coffee was laid out and a fire burned brightly. I turned aside to smother a yawn as we went in.

Mrs. Graham settled her cup upon her lap and looked over at Claudine. "How did you like the silk scarf, dear?"

Claudine frowned. "Scarf?" she echoed.

"Yes, the one the Culloms gave you for Christmas last month. I actually had a hand in picking it out." She waved a hand toward Mrs. Huntington. "Arabella and I, that is."

Mrs. Huntington said nothing. Noting the clenched hands in her lap, I suspected she was quietly seething over the aborted skirmish with her art-collecting rival.

"Oh! Why yes, it's a lovely scarf. I'd assumed Aunt Julia selected it."

Mrs. Graham shook her head. "She was feeling poorly and still had a number of gifts to shop for. We offered to help."

"That was quite kind of you. I appreciate it."

"It was no trouble," Beatrice Graham said. "I'm accustomed to doing all of the shopping for Jacob's business gifts as well. The man has no clue what to give people."

Arabella Huntington leaned forward and cast a pitying look in Mrs. Graham's direction. "That is no surprise, dear. Your husband's youth was a troubled one. He ran around with all sorts of undesirables, I hear. Not the sort of breeding one expects of a successful businessman."

Claudine and Anna exchanged a glance.

"That is all behind him now," Mrs. Graham said. Her twitching nose was the only indication of her pique. "Besides, Arabella dear, *your* husband has any number of skeletons in his closet. Jacob has told me of the underhanded deals and hostile takeovers the man orchestrates. But, as you are his *second* wife and married for only a few years now, I'm sure you don't know the worst of it, my dear."

The *dears* were flying fast and furious now. Was that a bit of color tingeing Arabella's cheeks?

What an odd pair—smooth as cream toward each other one minute, ready to go hammer and tongs the next. The men had been wise to fall back.

The girls' eyes were as wide as saucers now. I bit my lip to keep from laughing. "Shall I refresh your cup, Mrs. Graham?" I reached for the pot.

The gentlemen rejoined us soon after, and the evening reached a speedy, if not quite amicable, conclusion.

Once the guests were gone and the rest of us had exchanged our goodnights, I pulled Claudine aside. "I received a telegram from Chicago today. Anna's brother has been arrested."

Claudine sucked in a breath. "Poor Anna."

"As distressing as it is, she should be told. What I don't know is if it is better for you to tell her or for me to do so."

She bit her lip as she considered. "I'll tell her."

I stifled a sigh of relief. "Thank you, dear. Goodnight."

I checked the latches on the windows and doors of the first floor before retiring. This was Webb's job, but I wasn't going to take any chances. All was secure. Once I was dressed and ready for bed, I turned out my lamp and pulled the curtain aside to look out on the street and the park beyond. The night was bone-chilling cold. Few people would be disposed to linger out-of-doors. I let the minutes pass, watching. No sign of Lightfoot Lenny.

Did I dare to hope he was gone for good?

CHAPTER 9

*M*rs. Kroger, hobbling upon a cane and barking orders at the staff about the disposition of her luggage, left early for the train station on that cold, rainy morning, just as we were heading down to breakfast. Her goodbyes were stiff and formal, except for the quick embrace I saw her give Hattie in the foyer. She leaned in close to the girl and whispered in her ear. After that, she was gone.

I would have been quite content to stay indoors the entire day, but I had a fitting that afternoon. When I saw Jack's carriage pull up to the curb, I gathered my coat and hat and sought out the girls. Claudine was reading in the library.

"Where's Anna?"

She pointed to the settee behind a low bookcase. Anna was stretched out upon it, mouth slightly open, head propped against her arm, fast asleep. "Poor thing was up half the night, worried about her brother. I know she feels guilty for being here and not at home."

I sighed. "There wouldn't be anything she could do for him there."

Claudine gave a miserable nod. "Are you heading out now?"

"Jack's waiting. I should be back in time for dinner. Promise me that you two will not leave the house today."

She smiled. "Neither of us is tempted to go out, don't worry. But is there really cause for concern anymore? Lightfoot Lenny hasn't been seen since the night we arrived."

"I honestly don't know. We will continue to err on the side of caution."

I kept my nose to the carriage window again during our trip to R.H. Taylor's. Between the rainy gloom and the dying light of late afternoon, it was difficult to see. However, when we turned onto Ninth Street, a small hansom cab pulled away from the curb, waited for two carriages to pass, and traveled behind us at a discreet distance. A coincidence? I hadn't seen it at Iowa Circle. Still, it made me uneasy. I knocked on the panel behind the driver's seat.

Jack slid it open. "Yes, miss?"

"I think someone is following. Can you circle the block, just to be sure? And go a bit faster." I wanted to make sure it wasn't my imagination.

"Sure thing."

I felt the jolt as the horse stepped up to a brisk trot. I twitched aside the curtain of the back window again, just enough to see but not be seen. Yes, the hansom was picking up speed as well, splashing through puddles, weaving around slower vehicles in its path. I grasped the back of the seat as we took an abrupt right turn. I could hear the shout of an outraged driver that Jack had no doubt cut off in the process.

After the second right, Jack called back, "Is he still with us?"

"Yes!" I had to raise my voice, as the clattering of wheels and the drumming of rain made conversation challenging.

"You want me to lose 'im?"

"If you would," I called.

After a time, I lost track of what streets we turned down in our circuitous route to our destination. At one point, we slowed. Jack must have been checking for signs of pursuit. Finally, we pulled up to the curb, and he handed me out, holding an umbrella over my head.

"I wish I could have seen the occupant," I said. "Did you get a look?"

He shook his head. "I was trying to put distance between us, miss."

"It must have been Crill." I peered down the block. "You are sure he didn't learn our destination?"

"I'm sure, don't you worry. I cut through a private drive. He went right past. Never caught on. All too easy, actually." He scowled and shook his head. "Not the driest match in the tinderbox, that one."

Evidently, judging from Jack's annoyance, it was a source of manly pride to be challenged by a more worthy adversary. I was simply glad we had shaken him off for now.

Jack pulled out a toothpick—I'd swear it was the same one he'd been gnawing on the other day—and stuck it in his mouth. "Any idea when you'll be out, miss?"

"Only an hour, I hope."

He walked me to the entrance, keeping the umbrella over my head. "In case our man decides to search the nearby streets, I'll pull the carriage out of sight. Over there." He pointed to an alley a block down. "Come out of the left-side exit of the store instead of the main entrance when you're done. I'll be able to see you better. Then I'll bring the carriage 'round."

"Thanks, Jack. You be careful."

He grinned. "Don't you worry 'bout me. I got that cudgel, remember? I can take care of me'self."

The fitting took much longer than an hour, but I was pleased with the end result. The seamstress had cleverly employed a deep lace border to extend the hem and tucked in the waist while still keeping a bit of fullness at the skirt, helping to soften my angular frame. I turned to and fro in the three-way mirror, delighting in the folds of the sapphire silk in the play of the light. It was with some reluctance that I changed back into my sensible dark-gray worsted suit.

The seamstress had more trim to apply, but it was closing time. She promised to have it finished and delivered to Cullom's house by the next afternoon, despite it being a Sunday. That was cutting it close, as I was wearing the gown that evening, but it would have to do.

The night watchman waited patiently for me as I made my way to the left exit that Jack had designated. Once I'd stepped out, I heard the *click* of the latch as he locked up. The cold rain was coming down in sheets around the awning. I peered into the gloom. Where was Jack? It was past six already. I would have to hurry to make it back in time to change for dinner.

Ah—there was the carriage, with the distinctive smudge of white paint on its left fender, pulling away from the curb across the street and swinging around to my side. I pulled up my hood and hurried over, then stopped abruptly as the driver got out.

It wasn't Jack. It was the tall, dark, hulking form of Leonard Crill. My chest clenched.

I took a step back, scanning the empty sidewalk in hopes of passersby. He advanced, the rain dripping off the cap that shielded his eyes.

"Now then, Miss Hamilton," came the raspy voice, "we will have an uninterrupted conversation. Step into the vehicle."

My first impulse was to turn back to the store for aid, until I remembered the door was locked. My decision was made. I ran.

I heard his surprised shout as I bunched my skirts high in one hand and sprinted. By the time I had gained the corner, I realized the folly of running in a straight line. He would only wear me down and overtake me. I made an abrupt turn and darted into the street, dodging conveyances. I lost a shoe in a puddle and discarded the other that now only hobbled me. As I turned briefly to look back, I was nearly run down by a two-horse carriage, the driver's startled yell helping my pursuer locate me once again.

Straining for breath in earnest now, my stockinged feet wet, cold, and cramped, I ran alongside another coach to block my movements, then crawled under a wagon parked at the curb. I crouched behind a wheel. Heaven help me if the driver returned to move it in the next few minutes. I was soaked to the bone and so cold that I had to clamp a hand across my mouth to keep my teeth from chattering.

I strained to pick out his footsteps among the other sounds as I peered out between the wheel spokes. Would I recognize his form in the dim light? I considered the derringer in my reticule. It wasn't practical at a distance, as Cullom had pointed out, especially in such dim light. I didn't want to risk striking a bystander. But if Crill found my hiding place, the weapon was deadly enough at close quarters. I pulled it out and clutched it in trembling hands.

After what seemed an interminable interval with no sign of him, I ventured out of hiding and slipped down a side street, my gun hand dangling, concealed in the folds of my coat. The rain had subsided to a sporadic drizzle. Where was I? I cautiously approached the street signs on the corner, feeling as exposed as a hunted doe. I was on Sixth Street at D.

Wait. Sixth Street...that sounded familiar. I stuck the derringer in my skirt pocket, dug in my purse for Phillip Kendall's card, and tipped it toward the light. *National Hotel, Sixth and Pennsylvania Avenue.* If I remembered the city street layout correctly, I should be only a couple of blocks away. Going there for help seemed a better option than accosting a stranger, inquiring the location of a cabstand, and finding my way there. The latter course put me at greater risk of Lightfoot Lenny discovering me.

I'd be quite a sight for the hotel doorman and desk clerk, but I didn't much care. It was starting to sink in that something terrible had happened to Jack.

I turned toward the National Hotel, praying Kendall was there. I had to get back to Senator Cullom's house right away and make sure the girls were safe.

CHAPTER 10

The response to my bedraggled, unshod appearance was everything I could have expected. The frowns, raised brows, murmurs, and outright *tsks* of disapproval followed me as I traversed the marbled foyer and passed startled guests who lounged in red velveteen upholstered chairs. I assiduously avoided glancing at the gilded mirrors as I approached the front check-in desk. It was best not to know how bad it was. I clutched my damp coat close to my chest, kept my back straight and head high, and tried to still my chattering teeth as I inquired if Mr. Kendall was in.

The desk clerk snorted and looked me up and down. "And wot would Mr. Kendall be wanting with the likes of you, my good miss?"

"That is not your concern," I snapped. "Ring his room, if you please."

His lip curled. "We expect our guests and those who visit them to be *properly* attired. That includes shoes, you know."

"There has been a—a mishap." I shifted impatiently. We were wasting time. "Are you going to ring his room or not? Tell him Miss Hamilton is here to see him."

He muttered under his breath, picked up the receiver, and dialed. "Mr. Kendall? Sorry to disturb you, sir, but there is a"—he gave me another sharp look—"a woman asking for you. Not exactly, *er*, reputable-looking, but she's most insistent. Oh—her name?" He glanced at me.

"Hamilton," I hissed.

"Ah, yes. A Miss *Hamilton*, sir." He winced and held the receiver slightly away from his ear.

Judging by what happened next—I was quickly escorted to the manager's vacant office, offered a comfortable chair and a cup of hot tea—Kendall had given the clerk an earful.

I had not even reached for my tea when Phillip Kendall rushed in, then stopped, gawking at the sight of me. "Pen! What has happened?" He sat across from me in the small space, our knees nearly touching. "Are you all right?" He took my cold hands into his warm ones.

His concern on the heels of my ordeal nearly undid my composure. I took a shaky breath and pulled my hands away. "I will be. But I must get to Senator Cullom's house right away. If you're free, I could use the company, and I'll explain all this"—I gestured to my sad, sodden appearance—"along the way."

"Of course." He took off his jacket and put it around my trembling shoulders. "I'll call a cab and get my coat. I won't be but a moment."

He was as good as his word, and soon we were in the hansom and pulling away from the hotel. Kendall must have exhorted the driver to make it a speedy trip, as I required a firm handhold of the door during several turns.

I did not hesitate to relay the basics of my assignment, including my unfortunate encounters with Lightfoot Lenny. I wouldn't trust Phillip Kendall with my jewels—had I any, that is— but the man had proved himself trustworthy in an emergency, when I'd sorely needed an ally last summer.

Kendall gave a low whistle when I finished. "It's a wonder you were able to escape him. A dangerous man." His eyes softened as he regarded me. "But I have seen your ingenuity up close."

I was grateful the carriage was dark, for I felt my cheeks flush. Whether it was the compliment or the long, approving look of a handsome gentleman, I couldn't say. Neither comes my way very often. I cleared my throat. "His name is Leonard Crill. Have you heard of him?"

He snorted. "I rarely attend the monthly meeting of Reformed Criminals—so, no. I've never heard of him."

I chuckled. "I didn't mean it like that. You just seem to know a wide variety of people, that's all."

"Well, that is one man I do not care to know."

"There's nothing in his record that indicates he's ever killed anyone, but I fear for Jack."

"Jack? Oh, you mean the driver."

"Yes. Jack Porter. Cullom hired him to escort us these past few days and keep us safe. A resourceful fellow. When Crill was following us earlier today, Jack managed to lose him." Although not completely, it seemed. Crill must have found him while I was inside Taylor's. "So how did Crill come to be driving Jack's carriage tonight? Jack would never have voluntarily abandoned it. He must have overpowered him, perhaps even...killed him." I swallowed. Jack's body may have been inside the carriage. I didn't get close enough to see.

"That *is* worrisome. What can I do?"

I blew out a breath and returned from my dark thoughts. "I'm not sure, yet. First, I want to make sure the girls are safe. I honestly don't know what Lightfoot Lenny will do next. If he was willing to boldly take possession of Jack's carriage and chase after me..." My voice trailed off.

"Are the young ladies home alone?" Kendall asked.

"The staff is there. Claudine and Anna seemed safe enough at the time, but of course at that point, Leonard Crill had not been seen for days." I could kick myself now for leaving the house. For a dress? I didn't have that kind of vanity. "The senator may be home by now. What time is it?"

He pulled the watch from his vest. "Nearly seven."

"Heavens, they must be wondering where I am. The store closed an hour ago."

"About that," Kendall said, "perhaps this is an incident best kept from the young ladies, and especially from gossipy maids. You will, of course, inform the senator in private, but we should have a public story ready in the meantime." His mouth quirked. "Your appearance is rather—startling."

I grimaced. "Claudine—the senator's grandniece—is a sharp little thing. I'm not so sure anything we invent will fool her. But I agree we need a modified account of what transpired." The last thing I wanted was to give the Webbs unnecessary information until I was surer of them.

"Why don't we say that there was no sign of the carriage and you got caught in the rain? I came along and offered you a lift. Miss Pelley and Miss Zaleski can vouch for the fact that we'd already run into one another. It would be only natural for me to offer assistance."

"That part makes sense, but"—I glanced down ruefully at my stockinged feet—"how did I come to lose my shoes?"

"That's a bit more difficult to explain, I grant you. Perhaps the straps came apart when you inadvertently stepped into a deep puddle and the shoes were washed off your feet?"

I laughed. "Both of them?"

"Yes. Most unfortunate, do you not agree?"

In the end, I agreed to the absurd tale, for want of something better.

When we arrived at the Cullom house, Kendall insisted on stepping out of the coach first, to survey the area near the front walk and across the park for any sign of Leonard Crill. He returned after a few moments and opened the door. "All clear."

Before I could stop him, he reached for my waist and easily swung me down.

I cleared my throat awkwardly. "Thank you, Mr. Kendall."

His eyes took on a wistful expression. "I do wish you'd call me Phillip. After all, last summer you permitted me to call you Pen. It is only fair."

"Very well—Phillip. But let us keep that between us."

He gave a wide grin and tucked my arm in his.

Webb answered the door. His jaw hung slack for the barest of moments before he recovered himself and stepped back to let us in. "Miss Hamilton. The family has been worried about you."

"Where are Miss Pelley and Miss Zaleski?" I asked anxiously.

"I believe they are dressing for dinner, miss." His eyes flicked to Kendall. "And who are you, sir?"

Webb's somber, reproving tone didn't fluster Kendall in the least as he removed his hat and passed it to the butler. "A friend of Miss Hamilton's. Kendall's the name."

"I'm going up to change," I said quickly. The fewer people to see me in stockinged feet, the better. Really, this case was rife with absurd situations that had me running around without shoes far more often than I cared for. I hoped it would not become a habit. And to actually lose a pair...I didn't have that many shoes to begin with. "Can you show Mr. Kendall to the parlor, Webb? And tell the senator I will be down shortly. I wish to speak with him." Without waiting for a reply, I hurried upstairs.

Before proceeding to my room, however, I wanted to reassure myself that the girls were safe. I put an ear to their door and heard their murmur of conversation. *Thank heaven.*

Next, I began the formidable task of making myself presentable. The process involved a damp cloth from the wash basin to remove the dried mud and grime that adhered to my ankles, hands and wrists, then combing out my hair completely and putting it up in an expedient topknot twist, and last changing my clothes and groping for a spare pair of shoes. As I pulled what

I needed out of the wardrobe, I realized something was not quite right. I stood back for a better look.

Yes, something was definitely amiss. The armoire had been searched. A few of my more voluminous skirts had not been tucked back into place to hang down straight but were instead bunched against each other.

I ran to the hiding place for my lockpicks and logbook. They were still there, but someone had picked them up and put them back. The hairs were gone. A chill prickled the back of my neck. Someone—one of the staff—now knew who I was. Unless—the prickly sensation made its way down my entire spine at the thought—Lightfoot Lenny had been here.

I sat on the bed, rummaging in the pouch and spreading out the tools, counting everything to make sure. Nothing was missing. Once I had restored it all, I turned to the logbook. Just below my last entry of this morning was a scrawled note written in cheap lead pencil. The script was masculine and did not bother to follow the lines of the page.

You need a better hiding place, Miss Hamilton.

I did indeed. The cheek of the man, to jeer at me using my own logbook. But according to Frank's report, it was true to form.

Has been known to imprudently leave a taunting note for his victims.

I shuddered. The thought of Lightfoot Lenny having pawed through my belongings made me feel as if I had not quite scrubbed all of the dirt off my body.

It also made me more determined to catch him.

I took a few deep breaths to regain my composure and stowed the lockpicks in another hiding place to keep them from prying eyes. Of course, it was doubtful that any place was safe enough from Lightfoot Lenny. The logbook I decided to bring downstairs with me to show Cullom.

I stepped out into the corridor and nearly ran into Claudine and Anna, who had raised her hand to knock.

"Oh, Miss Hamilton, we're so glad you're back," Anna said.

Claudine nodded. "We feared you'd suffered a mishap."

I grimaced. "There was an unfortunate incident as I was leaving the store." I led the way to the staircase, the girls following me avidly. "I got caught out in the rain without the carriage."

"Where was Jack?" Claudine asked.

"I don't know. I suppose he was called away for something urgent. I know he wouldn't leave me stranded without a good reason. I'm sure he'll return later to explain." I prayed he would. I didn't hold out much hope, however.

"What did you do?" Anna asked.

"I tried to find a cabstand. The department store was locked up for the night, you see, so I couldn't turn for help there. Fortunately, Mr. Kendall was driving past, saw me, and stopped to offer assistance. He brought me back here, and I invited him in. He's in the parlor."

The girls brightened. "*Ooh*, we should have him stay for dinner!" Claudine exclaimed. "I'm sure Uncle Shelby won't mind."

Anna nodded. "It's the least we can do."

"No doubt Mr. Kendall will appreciate the kindness, though I cannot account for whatever Saturday evening dinner engagement he may already have. But you may ask him."

With a collective squeal, they turned toward the parlor.

"Is your uncle in the study?" I called to Claudine. She gave a little wave of assertion but didn't break her stride. I wondered if the girls' avid attentions would turn Mr. Kendall's head. No doubt he was used to such.

I tapped on the study door and opened it at the sound of a grunt.

Cullom's frown creased his forehead as he stood, but I couldn't tell if it was an expression of disapproval or concern. I was at least presentable now. "Miss Hamilton, Webb tells me you had some sort of...misadventure. And have collected a *gentleman?* in the process." He gestured to the chair across from his desk.

I sat, squeezing the book in my hands to maintain my calm. "It's a most distressing matter, Senator. Leonard Crill is still very much in the picture, even though we had not seen him for days. He nearly managed to kidnap me this evening, and I fear that Jack Porter is...dead."

"Dead!" He blew out a breath. "From the beginning, please."

I recounted the whole, starting when I noticed the vehicle following us to the department store this afternoon.

Cullom paled visibly during my account. "You were armed at the time?"

"Yes, but the derringer was in my reticule rather than my skirt pocket because of the dress fitting. As you have observed, such a weapon is not accurate at a distance, anyway." In this instance, a strong pair of legs was more useful than a gun.

"Why did you not contact the police at once, after you got away?"

"That would have taken time. I wanted to be sure of the girls' safety first and warn you about Crill. For him to do something so bold...I didn't know if he planned to come for the girls next."

Cullom exhaled. "Thank heaven Claudine and her friend are unharmed. I'm glad I took Huntington's advice and hired an extended staff. Having so many people underfoot no doubt deterred the man from coming to the house."

I shook my head and opened my logbook. "He has been here, today. Whether before or after he stole Jack's carriage, I do not know. This entire page was blank when I wrote my entry this morning." I passed it over.

His jaw clenched as he read. He handed back the book, then yanked the bell pull. "Send Webb to me, immediately," he barked at the maid who stepped in.

THE CASE OF THE RUNAWAY GIRL

"I don't want to alarm Claudine and Anna," I said. "I told them that Jack must have been called away to an emergency and left me stranded. I think it would be best to keep this to ourselves for now."

"Indeed. But how we are to protect them..." His voice trailed off.

"You will notify the police, of course."

He nodded, lost in thought.

"We must find Crill," I went on, "and learn who hired him and for what purpose. I can only think it is an enemy of yours, looking to get to you through Claudine."

He met my eye. "I have been considering the matter, believe me—" He broke off when the butler stepped into the room.

Webb gave a deferential bow. "Are you inquiring about dinner, sir? It should be ready momentarily." He shot a look in my direction. "We were waiting for Miss Hamilton. And now, I understand the other gentleman will be joining you?"

If Cullom was startled by the news, he didn't show it. Perhaps he was too angry at the thought of Lightfoot Lenny having gained entry into the house to care about an extra dinner guest. "Yes, yes. Naturally."

I was glad Kendall could stay. I wanted to show him the logbook and seek his opinion. Now that Jack was no longer here to help us, I felt quite alone. The responsibility weighed heavily.

Cullom inclined his head toward me. "Thank you, Miss Hamilton. I wish to speak with Webb in private. Tell Mrs. Webb to go ahead and serve the dinner. He and I may be a while."

I tucked the logbook under my arm. Webb's eyes shifted my way as I passed him and closed the door behind me.

CHAPTER 11

*I*t was a lively meal. The young ladies were so preoccupied with the handsome Phillip Kendall that they barely noticed Cullom's absence. Questions about their guest's background, profession, business in town, and especially his female companion from the tea room occupied most of the conversation. As I was curious about a great many of these things myself, I didn't bother to admonish their unladylike curiosity. Instead, I sat back and enjoyed the show.

Kendall was unflustered by the barrage and perfectly at his ease, an amused smile tugging at his lips. I knew from personal experience that he was a consummate liar. Still, I hoped to glean some gems of truth from his answers, based upon what little I already knew of him.

Kendall leaned back and fiddled with the stem of his water glass. "You ladies seem terribly young to be concerned with what a gentleman does for a living. Those sorts of questions are for one's papas, who will be screening the young fellows who come to call. After all, one must ensure that such men are proper suitors." He smiled. "But you are not quite at that stage."

The girls flushed and grew quiet.

Score one for the jewel thief.

After the soup was served, Claudine revived the interrogation. "Well then, what brings you to town, Mr. Kendall? And if you say *business*, then we are perfectly within our rights to ask what you do." She gave me a sideways look, a gleam in her eye.

I stifled a chuckle as I dabbed my lips.

Score one for the precocious young lady.

"Ah, but I am not here for business, Miss Pelley." He broke apart his dinner roll and reached for the butter dish. "A dear friend of mine, Congressman Walter Engels, is recovering from a long illness. I am here in town to visit him and escort his wife to various social engagements that had been arranged some time ago. A politician's wife should not stay out of the social sphere for long. People will talk."

I nodded, having seen it myself. What was it about a prolonged absence from society that spurred gossip? Whispers of financial misfortune, speculation about a dotty relative, or rumors of a marital scandal were common themes. As far as the latter, one would think that being escorted by a handsome man that is *not* one's husband would fuel such talk rather than quell it.

"So, the woman we met in the tea room is your friend's wife?" I asked.

"The same. Lydia Engels. Walter is most grateful that she has someone to accompany her. She had been tending him for weeks without much of a respite. She is particularly looking forward to our next outing tomorrow evening, the art auction at the Corcoran Gallery."

Anna unsuccessfully stifled a squeal. "We will be there as well! We are to be Senator Cullom's guests."

Kendall smiled. "How marvelous. It will be gratifying to know others there." He met my eye across the table. "The Washington crowd is not quite my set."

He was trying to tell me something, but I had no idea what.

"Are you looking to acquire any artwork at the auction, Mr. Kendall?" Claudine asked.

He laughed and waved a dismissive hand. "I haven't much time to sit in my residence and stare at whatever is hanging upon the walls. Mrs. Engels, however, is interested in a few items. She's especially fond of Moran's glasswork, though I fear the prices his vases fetch are beyond Walter's pocketbook." He leaned forward and whispered conspiratorially. "He wants me to keep his wife from bidding beyond a certain amount, you see. She doesn't know that." He put a finger to his lips and winked. "It is our secret."

Cullom didn't join us until after dinner, when we had retired to the parlor for coffee. He strode forward and shook hands with Kendall. "Please excuse me for being remiss in welcoming you to my home." He glanced back at Claudine and Anna, perched together on the settee. "Although I imagine the young ladies acquitted themselves admirably in my stead."

Kendall's eyes twinkled in good humor as the girls grinned widely. "Indeed, they have."

"And I want to thank you, sir, for coming to Miss Hamilton's rescue."

"My pleasure, Senator."

Claudine looked up with a frown. "Have you heard from Jack, Uncle Shelby? It's puzzling that he would simply abandon Miss Hamilton on a dark, rainy evening."

Anna nodded in agreement.

Cullom shifted in his chair. "Nothing yet, I'm sorry to say. I'll get to the bottom of it in the morning." He made a show of pulling his watch out of his vest pocket and consulting it. "I would say it is time for certain young ladies to retire for the evening."

The gentlemen stood politely as the girls said their goodnights.

As soon as they had left the room, Kendall nodded toward the book in my lap. "Is there something in your logbook you wish to show me? You've kept it with you the entire evening."

I suppressed a sigh. Of course he would recognize my logbook.

He had snooped in it just last summer. "I've already shown Mr. Cullom." I handed it to him, open to the page. "We believe this is Leonard Crill's writing, which means he got into the house today undetected, while I was out and the girls were here."

He grimaced and passed it back. "A taunt of sorts, I assume." He looked over at Cullom. "Does anyone know how he managed it?"

Cullom shook his head. "I have interviewed the butler. He asserts the doors were locked and no one has entered the house besides a couple of delivery boys who came to the back door—from the butcher's and grocer's, I believe. Both are well-known to the staff."

"Perhaps I could have a look around? I have some...experience with locks," Kendall said.

I raised an eyebrow. *Some* experience? His set of lockpicks was more extensive than my own.

He shot me a quick glance as if I had said it aloud. "I may be able to tell if any have been tampered with," he added.

Cullom looked at me, then Kendall, a quizzical expression on his face. "'Experience with locks,'" he echoed. "How do you two know each other? Are you a Pinkerton as well, Mr. Kendall?"

Kendall chuckled. "No, not at all. My father was a locksmith."

If true, that explained a few things. "Mr. Kendall and I met on my last case," I said. "He was of great assistance at the time. I would trust him...in this matter."

Kendall's eyes narrowed. Not exactly a *carte blanche* endorsement, and he knew it.

Cullom pursed his lips, considering. "Very well."

"I already checked the windows here in the parlor," Kendall said. "Nothing amiss. Shall we examine the remaining first-story locks?"

We accompanied Kendall on a survey of the first floor. The senator raised a speculative eyebrow when Kendall pulled out a jeweler's magnifying lens to inspect the casements. It is not every gentleman who carries such a tool in his evening jacket, after all.

Nothing seemed out of order with the first-story windows.

"We should survey the grounds next," Kendall said. "Miss Hamilton tells me Crill is an accomplished second-story man. Let us see how difficult it would have been for him to climb up."

As I had observed upon our arrival, the windows of the bedrooms the girls and I occupied at the front of the house were well away from any means of ascent, as the shrubbery here was nicely maintained. In the small yard behind the row house, however, the now bare-limbed wild cherry tree—probably the one Claudine and Hattie had climbed last summer—sprawled its sturdy branches toward the upper stories.

Kendall pointed. "The limbs close to a second-story window have been pruned, but the branches farther up have not. I imagine the gardener couldn't reach them. No doubt it wasn't considered a problem."

"You are saying he climbed not one, but *two* stories up this tree?" I asked.

Kendall nodded.

"Still, it's not terribly close to the house." I couldn't imagine traversing the space. There must be at least a four-foot gap.

Cullom, too, surveyed it with a skeptical eye. "You say a man could jump across that?"

"You'd be surprised." Kendall gestured toward a small window on the third story, closest to the tree limb. "Whose room is that?"

"One of the servants' bedrooms," Cullom said. "I don't know exactly whose."

"We should inspect the sill from the inside," Kendall said.

"All right, then." Cullom's mouth set in a grim line. "Let's go."

The window turned out to be to Hattie's room, which she shared with one of the new maids. We found heel marks by the sill and scoring at the latch.

My stomach clenched. "Surely these marks are not from today? It seems foolhardy to climb the tree in daylight."

Kendall shook his head. "I don't believe so. It has been raining all day, and the sill is dry."

So Lightfoot Lenny must have left those marks the night we'd arrived. A bold move on his part. Thank heaven I had taken precautions.

"How did he get in today, then?" Cullom asked. "Webb swears no one got past him or any of the staff."

Kendall shrugged. "The immediate question is what will you do now?"

Cullom rang for the Webbs.

"Move the maids to another room for tonight," he told the housekeeper. He turned to the butler. "Do you know how to fire a hunting rifle? Good. There is a locked chest behind the low bookcase in my study. Here is the key. Bring back the rifle and ammunition. You and I will be keeping watch here tonight, until we can get that tree trimmed tomorrow and a new lock installed." The butler hustled down the corridor.

"What are you going to do if you catch him?" I asked.

Cullom's jaw clenched. "I shall send for the police, and we'll have a chat while we wait. I want to know who hired him and for what purpose. I'm sure I'll think of more questions in the meantime."

I nodded. "Including the whereabouts of Jack Porter."

"Exactly."

"I'll stay with the girls tonight," I said.

He gave me a grim look. "Take your gun." Then he turned to Kendall. "We are in your debt, sir. Where are you staying? Can I arrange your transportation?"

"I'm at the National. But I'm willing to remain and keep vigil, if you wish."

"No, no, that won't be necessary. I believe our preparations are sufficient. Thank you all the same."

After my own brief but effusive thanks to Phillip Kendall—we would be seeing him tomorrow evening at the auction—I headed to my room in order to make my arrangements for the night.

I quickly changed out of my dinner dress of rose silk taffeta—not at all comfortable or conducive to quiet movement—and into my navy gabardine with pockets deep enough to hold my derringer and logbook. Writing a new entry regarding the latest developments this evening would help me stay awake.

Claudine was already clad in her nightdress when she opened her door to my quiet tapping. She put a finger to her lips. "Anna's asleep."

I looked over her shoulder. Anna lay upon the far bed, tumbled blonde hair peeking out from under the quilt. I heard a small snore. I doubted we would disturb her. "It's best if I keep watch here tonight," I whispered back. "I have troubling news."

Claudine's eyes widened as I described what we had discovered and a brief account of what really happened outside the department store.

She locked the door and helped me move the cushioned chair in front of it. "This is becoming a regular practice," she murmured.

I sincerely hoped not. A succession of nights sleeping in a chair was hardly beneficial to a lady's posture. "Your uncle will take additional precautions tomorrow." I settled myself in, pulling out my logbook and checking the derringer once more. "Will this light disturb you? I have an entry to make."

Claudine shook her head. "What sort of entry?"

"An account of events since my last notation." I grimaced. There was quite a lot to recount since this morning.

"Pen, what about Jack? Has he been..." she swallowed. "Killed?"

"I don't know. I hope not."

"Why is this man—Lightfoot Lenny—after me?" she asked. "Or is he after you? After all, it was you he chased today."

I'd been considering that very question. "The reasonable

conclusion would be that he wants me out of the way. I'm hindering his efforts to get to you. When he saw me alone, he took advantage of the opportunity to remove me as an obstacle."

She shivered. "To my mind, there is nothing *reasonable* about this. I envy you the ability to look at it so dispassionately."

I gave a wan smile. "My pulse was racing at the time, believe me. But if you can learn to control the sensations so they do not overrun your thoughts, you have a better chance of prevailing over the situation."

"How did you get away from him?" she asked.

I described what happened.

She listened with rapt attention. "That's dashedly clever," she said at last. "You believe he will keep trying?"

There was no point in sugar-coating it for the girl. "I do."

She sighed and was quiet for a while, staring at the dying fire. In the low light, I watched her dainty hands clenching the nightgown that hung from thin shoulders, saw the play of emotions cross her delicate face. No doubt she was assessing how, as small as she was in comparison to me, she would be equal to the physical challenge of eluding a pursuer.

I drew a breath, wanting to reassure her that there were ways to compensate for a size disadvantage, that she was more capable than she imagined.

But that was a discussion better suited for the morrow.

Claudine smothered a yawn.

"You should get some sleep, dear," I said.

With a weary nod, the girl climbed into bed and pulled up the covers.

The rest of the house grew quiet, the footsteps and murmurs overhead subsiding. I started from my chair at one point, however, when I thought I'd heard the creak of the back screen door. I waited, then relaxed at the sound of Mrs. Webb's murmur. With a shrug, I returned to my logbook, starting a fresh page to list my questions about the case.

Q: Who is Leonard Crill working for?

I assumed it was an enemy of Senator Cullom, even though the man staunchly claimed there had been no threat or demand made of him. What if Cullom was keeping back something? This wouldn't be the first time a client had become the greatest hindrance in a case.

Search Cullom's study, I wrote. I was glad I brought my lock-picks. I'd had a feeling they would come in handy.

But what if there was nothing to be found? That brought to mind another possibility, which I wrote down:

Q: Is Claudine really the target?

If Claudine was *not* Lightfoot Lenny's object, Anna and I were the only other possibilities. I was inclined to take myself out of consideration. I could think of no past case where someone with a grievance would go to such extremes.

Anna Zaleski seemed equally unlikely. True, the police suspected her family was involved with the anarchists convicted in the Haymarket bombing, but Leonard Crill was certainly not working for the police. They didn't have the funds to pay someone to trail Anna all the way to Washington, anyway.

Unless... I sat up straighter. Unless it wasn't the *police* who hired Lightfoot Lenny to follow Anna. What if the anarchists were behind it? If the Zaleski family had indeed collaborated with them, despite their protestations of innocence, the anarchists may have planned to snatch Anna in order to ensure her father and brother kept their silence under police interrogation. As distasteful a thought as it was, the idea was worth pursuing.

Learn more about possible Zaleski involvement with anarchists, I wrote. How I was to accomplish this when I was so far from the Pinkerton home office, I didn't know. Perhaps there was a local man that William Pinkerton could refer me to. It was a shame I didn't know any anarchists, I reflected. Then I caught myself. *What was I saying?* This line of work was having an odd effect on me.

In the course of my work, I had met a variety of people...on both sides of the law. I might not know any anarchists, but I *did* know a bomb-maker. When Frank and I were last in Washington, we had gone undercover for a month to break up a bomb-making ring. Frank had posed as a shady laboratory assistant for hire, and I was his secretary. We'd worked for...what was his name? I bit my lip as I wracked my memory. *Ah.* Lindquist. Artie Lindquist.

I shivered as I recalled the case. Bomb-making is a dangerous business. Frank and I had just wrapped up the evidence needed before the police were to step in when there was a horrible explosion. Lindquist had barely survived.

I wondered if he was still living in Washington. I didn't need to speculate as to whether he would help me. He owed me a favor. I'd saved his life.

CHAPTER 12

J was in a half-doze when the sound of a rifle blast from the upper floor brought me to my feet. The sound was followed by yells and running footsteps.

The girls bolted out of their beds, looking at me with terrified eyes.

I quickly shifted aside the chair and grabbed my gun. "Stay here. Lock the door behind me."

There were more footsteps overhead now. One of the maids shrieked and was quickly shushed. I took the servants' stairs two at a time. Cullom stood in the third-floor hallway, grasping the rifle and yelling at the butler. "What were you thinking, man? We were supposed to grab him, not shoot him without provocation." Webb looked down at his shoes and muttered something I couldn't catch.

"What's happened?" I asked.

Cullom gritted his teeth. "Crill was coming through the window when this ninny fired at him. Probably killed him."

I poked my head in Hattie's room. No one was there.

"He fell back out the window," Cullom said, noting my glance.

I winced. If the gunshot hadn't killed him, the two-story fall probably had. "We'd better go get him, bring him inside, and then send for the police."

But the latter turned out to be unnecessary, as a patrolman was already hurrying toward the house as we came out. "I heard a shot, Senator," he said, then tipped his cap briefly in my direction. "What's the trouble?"

"This way," Cullom growled. We followed him around to the backyard. There, in the dim moonlight, was the large form of Lightfoot Lenny. His breathing was labored, his face ghostly pale in sharp contrast to his dark beard and hair. He was attired in a close-fitting dark sweater and trousers. I picked up a crepe-soled shoe that had dropped nearby. The other was still on his foot.

"A second-story man, trying to break in, I 'spect," the patrolman said with a nod.

"More than a mere burglar, I'm afraid," Cullom said. "I'll need you to fetch a doctor and get a message to your district captain. The man may not have much longer."

"Did you shoot him, sir?" The policeman gestured toward the rifle still in Cullom's hand.

"My butler," Cullom said tersely.

"We should get him inside," I urged.

Cullom handed me the rifle and took Crill's shoulders while the patrolman took his feet. I ran ahead, opening doors, calling to Mrs. Webb to come help. The housekeeper hurried in with an armful of towels and draped the settee. Once the gasping man was stretched out, the patrolman left for the district station.

"How long will it take him?" I asked Cullom.

He grimaced. "It's about five blocks north, on U Street. But if he can commandeer a cab at this hour, it shouldn't be too long."

I watched Crill as he struggled to breathe, an ominous,

gurgling sound in the back of his throat. His eyes had not opened, and I despaired of him waking.

Cullom was not about to give up. "Crill? Crill, open your eyes! What were you doing in my house? Why do you mean harm to my family?"

Crill turned his head toward the sound. His eyes fluttered.

"Who hired you?" Cullom persisted.

"What have you done with Jack Porter?" I asked sharply.

That seemed to rouse him, and he opened his eyes. His glance darted back and forth between us. "Not...the plan."

"What wasn't the plan?" Cullom demanded.

But Crill paid him no heed. He looked searchingly in my face instead. "Why did he...? Webb... His voice trailed off as he lost consciousness again.

Within moments, the man had breathed his last. Cullom collapsed into a chair. "Now we'll never know. What did that mean, 'Why did he?' Was he that surprised at being shot while trying to break into a man's house?"

"Perhaps. He'd never been caught before. He was rather arrogant about his skills in that respect." I stood and smoothed my skirts. "I should go reassure Claudine and Anna." He nodded mutely.

The next several hours were a bustle of activity and upheaval as the doctor, police, and attendants came and went. Captain North, in charge of the second district, personally interviewed servants, guests, and family alike. I was the last one he called into Cullom's study.

He was an older man with an iron-gray, grizzled beard and creased, hooded eyes. His navy tunic was spotless, though it stretched a bit around his middle when he sat.

"Now then, Miss"—he consulted his notepad—"Hamilton?"

I nodded.

"You are employed by the Pinkerton Agency and are working

in that capacity for Senator Cullom?" His tone was neutral. I heard no incredulity there. Perhaps lady detectives were a more common phenomenon in Washington.

"Correct, sir."

"I see. Well, I have most of the story of the shooting from the senator and butler, but I understand there was a separate incident yesterday evening, involving you and the dead man, Leonard Crill. Tell me about that."

I related what had happened outside the department store and how I had evaded my would-be abductor—was that a flash of approval I glimpsed on North's face?—along with the subsequent proof that Crill had been in the house at some point that day. I fetched my logbook to show him.

He glanced at it, scribbling rapidly on his pad and shaking his head. "Someone is going to a great deal of trouble to threaten the senator."

"Has Mr. Cullom told you who he thinks may be behind it?" I asked. "He has not been forthcoming with me."

North gave me a stern look. "Senator Cullom would not withhold crucial information when his household is in jeopardy. The notion is absurd."

I wondered how absurd it really was and silently vowed to search the study at my first opportunity.

North stood. "Thank you for your account, miss. I have all I need."

"Will you be looking for Jack Porter?" I asked, also standing. "He wouldn't simply abandon me like that. I fear he has come to harm."

"Indeed, we will. I'll send out descriptions of him and his vehicle to the other precincts as well." He clucked his tongue. "It's a shame the sneak thief has died. All that information lost to us."

"Will you continue the extra patrols past the senator's house? We don't know if Crill was working with anyone."

"For a few more days, perhaps, but we are short-staffed," he said. "I cannot spare the men indefinitely."

"Well, then, we shall have to wrap up this matter quickly."

He narrowed his eyes. "I have no control over how you conduct your affairs, miss, but I would advise you to proceed carefully."

I waited with the girls in the library as Crill's body was taken away. Once the front door was shut and everyone had finally gone, Anna turned to Claudine. "What a relief it's over."

Claudine gave a distracted nod.

"It seems mild enough for a walk out-of-doors," I said, collecting my shawl. "Care to join me, Claudine?"

The girl eagerly ran for her jacket, and soon we were breathing in the crisp air and walking in companionable silence.

"Do you really think we have nothing more to fear, now that Lightfoot Lenny is dead?" Claudine finally asked.

"Caution would be wise," I said. "Someone hired the man, and we have not been able to determine who."

Claudine plucked at her jacket sleeve. "I fear I am not as strong or as resourceful as you. I would be quickly overpowered should someone mean me harm."

"You underestimate yourself. You are an active young lady. You grew up on a farm and are accustomed to exertion." I gestured to Cullom's backyard tree, just visible behind the houses as we turned the block. "You told me you and Hattie climbed that last summer. How high did you get?"

"Nearly to the top." Claudine chuckled. "Mrs. Kroger had a fit when she saw us."

"Well, I would not be capable of such a feat. You may be small, but that has its advantages. You are more agile and can squeeze into compact spaces. Frank Wynch told me how you were able to escape the cab and leave him behind on a Chicago street."

"That seems ages ago."

"You may also be able to slip out of ropes more easily."

Her eyes went wide. "You think he intended to kidnap me and tie me up?"

I nodded. "It seems more likely than...doing away with you." I hesitated, but she seemed perfectly calm, so I went on. "Otherwise, whoever is behind this would have hired a sharpshooter and accomplished his purpose while concealed at a distance, on any number of occasions. But what does he do instead? He hires an ex-convict known for slipping undetected in and out of houses. Which tells me that kidnapping was the plan."

"Do *you* know how to get out of ropes?"

"I've done it once." I winced at the memory. "I can show you what I know."

She looked at me with a steady eye. I saw no fear there. "Let's go. I want to start now."

We procured a length of rope from the gardener's shed and retired to my room.

"You'll first want to get out of the binding around your wrists," I said. "Once your hands are free, you can work on your other bonds. If you're conscious when someone ties you, you can try holding your hands in front of you, this way." I formed two fists, the knuckles of each hand pressed together. "Your captor may not notice that there is a bit of space between your wrists because your hands are in the way, see?"

She nodded and practiced the position.

I shared other tips—tensing one's muscles so that the bonds are looser when one relaxes, taking a deep breath to expand the chest if one is strapped to a chair, slipping off shoes to facilitate an escape from ankle bonds. Then I tied the rope around her wrists. I kept it looser until she improved. We did it several times, and I could see, by the determined look on her face, that her confidence was growing.

Finally, we rested from our exertions, she sitting cross-legged on the floor in front of the fire, me on the rocker.

"You've been very quiet," I said. "Are you concerned about the redness on your wrists? It should subside. Although I don't know if the marks will be gone by the auction tonight." I grimaced. I should have considered that before we'd started.

"I'm not worried about that," she said. "I have elbow-length opera gloves to match my gown."

"So, what is on your mind?"

"I—I felt a moment of panic, the first time you bound me more tightly." She shivered. "A most uncomfortable sensation."

"That can be controlled, with practice," I said. "You need your wits about you. And it may not come to that at all. Something might be at hand that you can put to use to elude capture to begin with—a pan of scalding water, a pair of scissors, a chair."

She nodded, still staring into the fire.

We started at the knock on my door.

It was Anna, holding a long, white box marked *R.H. Taylor & Co.* "Miss Hamilton, this just arrived for you. It must be your gown for tonight! Let's see—" She stopped, pointing at the rope. "What are you doing with *that?*"

Claudine quickly got up. "Oh, it's just an experiment."

I checked the time. "You ladies should start getting ready. I'll show you the dress once I have it on, all right?"

Claudine gave me one last look over her shoulder, a smile tugging at her lips.

Once they had closed the door behind them, I threw the rope in a drawer so as not to scandalize the staff, retrieved my lock-picks, and hurried downstairs. I hoped the senator had already gone up to change for the evening.

The study door was closed and locked, as expected. I knocked and waited. No response. I checked the corridor. When I was sure no one was nearby, I pulled out my tools. The man's door lock was nothing special. I had it open in a moment.

I took a breath once I was inside the room and had secured the door. I didn't bother going through his unlocked file cabinet.

From what I had observed of the senator thus far, he was a cautious man who didn't trust easily. Having new servants in the house would cause him to be even more circumspect. If there was an important document or letter that he wanted to keep from prying eyes, he would have locked it in his desk.

The desk lock was newer, as if he'd had it replaced recently. It took some trial and error with my picks before I had it open. I eyed the mantel clock. Six thirty. I would have to hurry. Not only did I need time to change before we were to leave for the auction, but Cullom might return shortly. Men do not need as much time as women to change into evening attire.

The desk drawers contained the usual bank statements, business reports, and a few letters from constituents, though I imagined he kept the rest in his office downtown. I paid particular attention to his personal correspondence. Nothing unusual. No mention of Claudine at all. I bit my lip and glanced at the clock again—twenty minutes had passed. With a sigh, I restored the piles and closed the drawers. The shallow center drawer, however, wouldn't completely close. I reached in to dislodge whatever was in the way.

But it was not a pencil or a piece of paper. It was a lever. I felt a little thrill of excitement as I pushed.

A small, hinged panel, built into the decorative trim between the drawers, popped open. My hands trembled as I removed a cheap envelope of plain white paper. The senator's name was written upon the front in block letters. There was no address beneath.

Footsteps. Heart in my throat, I closed the panel, pocketed both the envelope and my tool pouch, and slipped behind the curtains drawn across the French doors. When I heard the key in the lock, I unlatched the glass door behind me and opened it just enough to squeeze out—I didn't want a draft fluttering the curtains and giving me away—then quietly pushed it closed.

I found myself on the back patio, blinking to adjust to the sudden darkness. Fortunately, the kitchen door was only steps away. I let myself in, much to the surprise of one of the new maids scrubbing the sink.

"Just getting a breath of air," I called over my shoulder as I whipped past her and climbed the servants' staircase. Time to change for the auction...*after* I looked at what was inside that envelope.

Once I was safely back in my room, I brought it over to the nightstand lamp. Inside was a single sheet of stationery, plain and unremarkable, written in the same crude block lettering.

IF YOU VALUE THE CONTINUED HEALTH OF YOUR FAMILY YOU WILL ALLOW THE BILL TO DIE IN COMMITTEE. THIS IS A FRIENDLY WARNING.

The note was undated. When had it been delivered? Before we arrived or more recently than that? I read it again. *ALLOW THE BILL TO DIE IN COMMITTEE.* Senator Cullom no doubt oversaw and voted upon many bills, but after the recent dinner party with Huntington and Graham, it seemed the most contentious one was the railroad bill. What had Claudine called it? Yes—the Interstate Commerce Act. Had Huntington made the threat? He seemed the most likely candidate. *I have a few other tricks up my sleeve,* he'd said. He was widely known for dodgy maneuvers that danced upon the edge of legality as angels—or devils—dance upon the head of a pin. His influence and resources stretched widely. And yet, why risk it? It could so obviously be traced back to him.

Of course, others had much to lose as well. Would one of the other railroad magnates be willing to take such drastic measures? Cullom would know. I would have to confront him with what I found. I hoped he wouldn't dismiss me on the spot for breaking into his study.

I didn't know it at the time, but Cullom would have greater cause to fire me by the end of the evening.

CHAPTER 13

$\mathcal{O}$ur carriage joined the other vehicles that waited in the queue along Pennsylvania Avenue to discharge passengers in front of the Corcoran Gallery of Art. As we crept along, the young ladies kept their faces to the window, watching the top-hatted gentlemen and bejeweled ladies in fur stoles who proceeded up the steps. Additional lanterns lit up the entrance, where a banner was strung across the upper pillars: CHARITY AUCTION TONIGHT.

Finally, it was our turn. Webb—pressed into service as our driver at the last minute when the original hired cabbie showed up reeking of bourbon—handed us down.

"I'm sorry to say it, Webb, but I'll want you to wait 'round the corner with the other drivers," Cullom said. "Don't know exactly how long we will be staying."

Webb nodded with an aggrieved sigh. "Very good, sir."

Cullom extended his arm to his grandniece.

She took it with a wide smile. "I am so excited, Uncle Shelby. I've never been to anything near so grand."

He chuckled. "I must say, seeing such an event through your

eyes, my dear, lends a refreshing slant to the evening. Shall we?"
They led the way. Anna and I followed.

Attendants waited in the vestibule, checking invitations and
distributing printed brochures of the artwork up for auction. I
glanced through mine as I climbed the stairs to the main picture
gallery. It was quite a list of offerings. I wondered which piece
Phillip Kendall's companion was at risk of overbidding upon.

As if conjured by my thoughts, I nearly bumped into Kendall
when I reached the top of the burgundy-carpeted stairs. "Good
evening, Mr. Kendall."

"Ah, it is good to see you, Miss Hamilton. You are looking
lovely this evening." His eyes were warm and admiring as he
glanced over my gown and the pearl circlet that Claudine and
Anna had insisted upon affixing in my hair. I felt my cheeks flush.
Vanity, thy name is woman. Or was that frailty? Sometimes they
were one and the same.

I looked over his shoulder, but there was no sign of his
companion. "Where is Mrs. Engels?"

He nodded toward the sweep of railing and open space
beyond, where clusters of people chatted and sipped champagne.
"I left her to socialize while I take care of her wrap."

At last I spied the lady, near the Octagon Room. She was
attired in a gown of crimson lace over ivory silk, its décolletage
plunging as low as good taste permitted. She stood with a group
of matrons, laughing and nodding over their brochures.

Senator Cullom approached us. "Ah, Kendall, we had quite an
eventful night after you left."

"So I heard," Kendall murmured. "The man has died, as I
understand."

Cullom's brow furrowed. "Dashed butler. A bit too enthusiastic, shot the man on sight."

"How unfortunate. Did the intruder say anything before
he died?"

"Nothing revelatory." Cullom sighed. "At least we have nothing more to fear from that quarter."

I recalled the anonymous note in Cullom's desk, now concealed with my logbook and picks. I wasn't so sure it was over. "Where are Claudine and Anna?" I craned my head to survey the press of people. Most of the guests were here on the upper level, helping themselves from the silver platters of canapes offered by the hired waitstaff that circulated the open area. "I don't see them."

"They were in the sculpture room downstairs, last I noticed," Cullom said. He turned back to Kendall. "Would you and Mrs. Engels care to join us during the auction? We have two extra seats available in the second row."

Kendall gave a little bow. "That is most generous of you. I will consult with the lady."

"Excuse me," I murmured. "I'm going to catch up to the girls."

Claudine and Anna were standing at the foot of the stairs, comparing art brochure pages with Mrs. Huntington and Mrs. Graham.

"Oh, Miss Hamilton!" Anna exclaimed as I approached. "We were just about to go up to the main picture gallery, where the items are on display."

Claudine nodded and pointed to a page in the catalog. "Including *The Carnival* by Fanshaw. Everyone is talking about it."

I frowned. "Fanshaw…isn't he the one who paints…scantily clothed subjects?" Hardly suitable for delicately reared young ladies, though perhaps neither girl fell into quite that category.

Beatrice Graham snorted into her handkerchief as Arabella Huntington explained. "He does enjoy a bit of notoriety for his oils. But never fear, *Miss* Hamilton." She pursed her lips and looked me up and down. "*The Carnival* is one of his pastels. Those deal in…appropriately attired subjects."

The woman must think me a prudish spinster. I firmly suppressed the laugh that threatened to bubble out. Generally speaking, my comportment is above reproach, but a certain Parisian summer back in '74 taught me that I am not a prude at heart. Mama would have been scandalized to learn that story.

Mrs. Graham led the way to the main picture gallery, the girls close at her heels. Mrs. Huntington and I followed at a more leisurely pace. Here, perhaps, was an opportunity to learn how desperate her husband might be in regards to Cullom's railroad bill. Would he go to the extreme of sending Cullom an anonymous threat? Did he intend to have Claudine kidnapped? And now that his hired henchman was dead, had he lined up another, waiting in the wings?

"I don't see your husband, Mrs. Huntington," I said.

"Collis has no interest in modern art. And he has had a great deal of work keeping him occupied lately."

"I imagine a successful railroad man such as he has many demands upon his time. Do you two still plan to head back to New York this week?"

The lady's jaw clenched. "Sadly, no. It has been a more difficult task to deal with this issue of commerce regulation than he had anticipated. But I mustn't speak out of turn. You are a friend of the senator, after all."

"I'm an employee of the senator," I corrected. "His grandniece is in my charge. Besides, I have no political view on the subject."

Mrs. Huntington shook her head. "I envy you the luxury of being apolitical. As Collis's wife, it is impossible."

I gave her a sideways glance, noting her splendid emerald satin gown with deep lace trim and the sparkle of green gems at her throat and ears. The whole was extremely flattering to her peaches-and-cream complexion and dark hair.

It seemed to me the lady had traded one sort of luxury for another.

We stepped into the gallery and approached the tables where the paintings were displayed on easels.

I thought back to the bits of information I'd gleaned through

Cullom's study door at the dinner party. "I take it this railroad bill has been in the works for quite a while."

She nodded. "You mean the Interstate Commerce Act. Yes, it has been the senator's project for more than a year."

"But I understand there is more than one version of the bill." I recalled Graham's words: *You must admit that his version is at least better than Reagan's.*

"Indeed. A key difference between the two has to do with how the new rules would be enforced. The senator's bill provides for a board of commissioners with the power to regulate interstate traffic. Congressman Reagan's version consists of statutory provisions, which would mean enforcement rests with the federal courts."

"Which does your husband prefer?"

Her eyes narrowed. "Neither option is acceptable," she snapped. "That is what occupies him so. He has been exceptionally distracted lately. But I have already spent more time on the subject than I care to." She veered toward a table to our left. "If you will excuse me, Miss Hamilton, I want a closer look at the Siebert watercolor."

"Of course," I murmured at her back.

Claudine and Anna were already in their seats and engaged in an animated discussion with Phillip Kendall and Mrs. Engels, who sat beside the girls. Gone was the lady's sulky demeanor of the tea room. She smiled at me as she indulgently tipped her head to listen to the enthusiastic chatter of Claudine and Anna. Perhaps Kendall had explained the situation to her, and she no longer considered me a rival for his attentions.

Speaking of attention, Kendall himself was paying little heed to the conversation. True, his torso was turned toward the ladies, but he frequently glanced over his shoulder as people in the crowd moved about. My heart sank when I realized his eyes followed the wealth of gems on display—pearl-crusted tiaras, ponderous sapphire pendants, flashy diamond bangles that caught the light as the wearers tugged at gloves, waved to acquaintances, and plied their fans in the warm room. So, Phillip Kendall was still up to his old tricks.

Then he went rigid, and I followed his gaze to the right side of the room. A comely, blonde-haired woman, attired in a close-fitting peach satin, was bending to examine a pastel. Had it been any man but Kendall, I would have ascribed his absorption to the full swell of bosom that such a posture offered. More likely what had caught his attention, however, was the equally stunning, multi-strand pearl choker at her throat. The pearls looked to be perfectly matched as they caught the light.

I took a seat beside him, and he immediately turned from the sight. "Ah, Miss Hamilton. See anything you like?" He gestured toward the tables.

I narrowed my eyes. "There have been a few items of interest. There is no doubt about that."

Senator Cullom, smelling suspiciously of cigar smoke, joined us soon after. "Somebody or other pressed this on me." He impatiently waggled the bidding placard in his hand. "Don't know why. I've no intention of buying anything for the house without Mrs. Cullom's approval. I'd never hear the end of it." Still clenching the placard, he reached up to tug at his collar. "Lord, it's stifling in here."

"Sir," Kendall said, reaching across me to still the senator's arm, "I'd be careful how I'd wave that around, if I were you."

"Hmm?" Cullom frowned.

Kendall nodded toward the auctioneer, who was pounding his gavel to settle the crowd. "You may end up bringing something home, after all."

Cullom's brow cleared, and he chuckled. "That would not do." He passed me the placard. "Here, Miss Hamilton, you'd better hold on to it." I smiled and kept it in my lap.

Completing our row were the Grahams and Mrs. Huntington. Polite introductions were made all around. The wives sat side by side, each holding a numbered placard. As Jacob Graham took his seat next to the senator, he winked. "I see the competition for the watercolor is about to commence," he mock-whispered. "Let us hope the bid doesn't go too high. They will become mortal enemies, and my purse is sure to be the poorer for it."

Mrs. Graham gave him a sharp glance. Her hands twitched as she grasped the placard more tightly. I suspected the lady was sorely tempted to whack her husband with it.

The gavel came down once more, and we turned our attention to the auctioneer.

By the auction's end, it seemed a satisfactory result for our group. No one accidentally bid on anything, Lydia Engels got her glass vase for a modest amount, and although Mrs. Graham and Mrs. Huntington were each outbid for the Siebert watercolor by an elderly gentleman in the back row, both women seemed content with what they'd bought instead. I wondered if those two simply enjoyed the competitive nature of the enterprise.

Our host for the evening, assistant curator Mr. Brixton, stepped up to the auctioneer platform. "Ladies and gentlemen, thank you all for coming. Your generosity will go far in helping us raise enough funds to build a new wing. Then we can sponsor more up-and-coming artists and expand our gallery offerings. A coffee-and-dessert table has been set up in the Octagon Room. Please, feel free to partake." He stepped down to polite applause.

Cullom frowned and pulled out his watch. "It's getting late. Should we call it a night, ladies?"

I was inclined to agree, but Claudine and Anna shook their heads vigorously.

"Just a bit longer, Uncle Shelby?" Claudine wheedled.

Senator Cullom glanced at me. I shrugged. "Perhaps long enough to sample the dessert table."

He chuckled. "Far be it for me to come between ladies and their sweets."

The girls headed for the Octagon Room, while Cullom made for the terrace, already reaching for his cigar case. I went downstairs with some of the other patrons, eyeing the figures in the Sculpture Hall and the Hall of Bronzes, but in actuality looking for Kendall and Mrs. Engels. They had seemed to slip away. I was surprised that Kendall, at least, would not have said goodbye. I didn't know when I would be seeing him again, and the thought unsettled me in a way I couldn't explain.

I caught a glimpse of him outside the cloakroom and hurried to catch up. Lydia Engels, already wearing her wrap, was rummaging in her purse. She had her back to Kendall, who had thrown his own coat over his arm and was gallantly helping two other ladies with their wraps. I recognized one of them as the same buxom, blonde-haired woman who had held his attention before.

Kendall had not noticed me approach, and what happened next stopped me in my tracks. As he settled her collar and fussed with the scarf at her throat, his fingers lingered. He withdrew his hands, reaching quickly for his own coat still over his arm, and gave a bow to the ladies, who smiled and left.

It was done so quickly and expertly that I nearly doubted my own eyes. But the gleam of pearls, before the strand was hidden between his hands, then slipped inside his coat, was unmistakable. He had stolen the pearl choker right from the young lady's neck. And she had no idea.

I stood there, in an agony of indecision, as Kendall settled his coat over his shoulders, took Mrs. Engels's arm, and left.

"Pen," said a strained voice near my elbow. I jumped. Claudine stood beside me, face pale and drawn. "I can't find Anna."

CHAPTER 14

e checked the ladies' retiring room first before seeking out Senator Cullom. The female attendant was just about to lock up.

"Have you seen a girl in here recently?" I asked. "About this tall"—I held my hand up to my chin—"blonde hair piled in ringlets, wearing an aquamarine-colored gown?"

The woman nodded. "Jus' a little while ago. She asked for help getting out a stain. Dropped a bit of meringue on herself." She pointed to her bodice. "I had just the thing for her—Mrs. Nickerson's Cleaning Tonic. Works wonders on any mark."

Claudine waved an impatient hand. "Once you cleaned the stain...did you see where she went?"

"I didn' even get the chance to use it. By the time I was back from the pantry with the bottle, the young lady was gone." The woman clucked her tongue. "Girls these days. Not a lick of patience."

Cullom was collecting our coats when we caught up to him and explained what had happened. His brow darkened. "Webb is bringing the carriage 'round. Perhaps Anna is already out there."

"Without her cloak?" Claudine pointed to the light gray wool in his arms. "That's hers."

"I'll go see," I said. "Wait here." I dodged the last few patrons along the front steps as they made their way to waiting vehicles. Webb straightened at my approach and touched his cap. "Ready to go, miss?" His eyes narrowed. "Where's the senator?"

"Webb, have you seen Miss Zaleski?"

"Why no, miss, I haven't. Is something wrong?"

My throat grew too tight to answer. I pulled open the door and stuck my head in the carriage. Empty. I turned and ran back into the gallery.

Cullom promptly sought out the assistant curator, who recruited the night watchman to help us search. By then, everyone else had gone home, so only the footsteps of the five of us rang upon the floors.

No matter how absurd the location—or how distressing to contemplate—we looked in it, calling out all the while. The guard unlocked doors, storage bins, even deep cabinets. We went into the basement and looked under tarpaulins. Every studio was searched, though no one should have been able to get in without a key. Claudine grew paler by the minute and clutched my arm so hard it was getting sore. I could feel her tremble.

We'd run out of places to search and had reached the back door of the building. Cullom tried the knob, but it was locked. "What's beyond?"

"A loading dock, sir, to bring in supplies and such."

"Well, man, don't just stand there. Unlock it!"

Once it was open, Cullom impatiently took the lantern from Mr. Brixton and led the way. "Watch your footing," he said. "There isn't a railing."

We groped our way cautiously. The platform was elevated, to make it easier for an expressman's cart to pull up and unload.

We began shoving boxes aside.

Claudine stiffened and picked up a long, white silk glove that had snagged upon a wooden crate. "Look! This is Anna's."

Cullom came closer with the lantern. "Are you sure? It could be any lady's."

She shook her head. "I'm sure. See the light-blue rhinestone buttons? I helped her sew those on, to match her gown."

"It looks as if someone forced her back here and took her away in a conveyance," I said. "We should find out if anyone saw a coach pull around to the dock tonight."

"Now we'll never find her!" Claudine turned her face into her uncle's jacket and began to sob.

As one might imagine, it was a long night. Cullom sent us home with Webb while he awaited the police at the gallery. Naturally, Claudine resisted going to bed, though she looked ready to drop. "I want to know the moment they've found Anna," she wailed.

"I promise to wake you if there's any news."

She gave me a doubtful frown.

I put my hands on my hips. "Have I ever lied to you, Miss Pelley? Now, to bed."

She went.

Once I had checked for myself that all the locks were secure, I changed out of my evening gown into my dark dress with the deep pockets and brought my logbook down to the library to wait.

My log entry was naturally an extensive one, and yet no one had arrived by the time I was done. I glanced at the mantel clock as I put another log on the fire. One o'clock.

I resettled myself and let my mind drift. If Leonard Crill were still alive, I would have credited him with Anna's abduction. But with him dead, who was acting in his place? How would such a person manage to take the girl without attracting attention? This was a special event for Washington's elite art collectors and other notables. A rough-and-tumble, hired criminal would stand out by a mile.

I turned my thoughts to Anna. Why was *she* taken and not Claudine? I'd been so sure, after finding the letter in Cullom's study, that his grandniece was the target. Even the *why* of it was straightforward—to sabotage the passage of the Interstate Commerce Act.

Anna's abduction, however, made no sense. Could the kidnapper have taken the wrong girl? It seemed unlikely. The young ladies did not resemble each other at all. Anna was pale-haired, taller, and of a stockier build. And no new ransom note after Anna's disappearance had come to light, either at the gallery or here at the house.

Supposing the letter to Cullom was an empty threat, I'd have to dust off my earlier theory of the anarchists in Chicago wanting to insure the Zaleski family's continued silence. Which meant I had to talk to Lindquist as soon as possible.

If I could find him.

I must have dozed before the fire. The sound of the library door opening jolted me awake. Cullom stood in the doorway, his cheeks pinched and pale, his glare as black as thunder. "We have to talk, Miss Hamilton."

I stood and shook out my skirts with nervous hands. *Here it comes.* "Sir," I began, working to keep my voice steady, "I'm so sorry that Anna has been taken. I did not anticipate her being a target, and with the death of Leonard Crill, I—"

"I am not holding you responsible for the poor girl being missing," he interrupted. "I'm as surprised as you are." He crossed the room and came within arm's reach. "I have just discovered that you broke into my study and stole a letter." He held out a hand. "I want it back."

I slipped it out of my logbook and passed it over, wondering what made him look for it now. "Do you believe it's connected with Anna's disappearance?"

He didn't answer as he frowned over the note by the light of the fire, not even troubling to turn up the lamps.

I tried again. "I sensed you were holding something back. For Claudine's sake, I had to learn what it was."

Still, he didn't look up or acknowledge me in any way.

"Perhaps—perhaps I should have pressed you further, before taking the surreptitious route," I added contritely.

He looked at me then. "You don't do anything by halves, do you?" He sighed. "I suppose I should have shown it to you. But I did not see the threat as genuine." His expression sobered. "Not until I saw Leonard Crill climbing in my third-story window, that is. And now, Anna's gone, even though Crill is dead. What in blazes is going on?"

"When did the letter come, and by what means? Messenger? It could not have been by post. There is no address on the envelope."

He ran a weary hand over his head. "It didn't come to the house. It was inside a book I'd left in the staff lounge at the Capitol building. A congressional page recognized the book as mine and brought it to me, not knowing the letter was inside."

"When was this?"

"Mid-December."

Long before we'd come.

"Where is this lounge?" I asked. "Who has access to it?"

"It's just beyond the Senate dining room. Back in mid-December...hmm...hard to say who was there. It would have been quite busy then. We had just resumed work on revising the bill so it could pass both the House and Senate. Prior to that, each of us had our own version of the law, and there were significant differences to reconcile." He sighed and murmured, half to himself, "Here it is mid-January, and the opposition continues."

"So the area is for staff only?"

Cullom shook his head. "We're rather cramped for space. Most of us don't have offices right there in the building, so we use whatever meeting areas we can find. All sorts of people come and go without question—fellow senators, other lawmakers, newspapermen, lobbyists, even family."

No help there. "Any idea who left the note? Do you recognize the handwriting? It looks disguised."

He shook his head. "The hand is unfamiliar. If the threat is an earnest one, there are only a few people who have enough at stake to be so desperate."

"Railroad moguls such as Collis P. Huntington, you mean?" I prompted.

"Yes, but he certainly isn't the only one."

"Was he in the Capitol building around that time?" I wondered why I was still pursuing this angle, when it was Anna who was missing. For the sake of being thorough, I supposed.

"Oh, certainly. He has the ear of several lawmakers and hasn't been shy about airing his grievances over the bill. He stepped up his efforts during that time, when it became apparent that the bill was gaining momentum."

"What about Jacob Graham? His wife mentioned them being in town these past few months. He has railroad interests, does he not?"

"Only a partial interest, in the C&O," Cullom said. "He helped Huntington finance the Peninsula Extension of the line. It's more efficient to have a hand in how one is supplied, you see. But his primary interest is in the shipbuilding and dry-dock company that he owns. Down in the Chesapeake area. With the new extension, more West Virginia coal reaches his yards now."

"So he does have a stake in this," I said.

Cullom shrugged. "He holds the same view as Huntington regarding regulation, certainly, but he has not been on the Hill trying to fight it. He has other fish to fry."

"Could a *group* of railroad owners have hatched such a scheme?"

He frowned. "It would be foolhardy in the extreme to collaborate to carry out such a threat. Someone would talk. And I haven't received any anonymous notes besides the one."

"Good point. And none of this makes sense when it is Anna who has disappeared. What have the police been able to determine?"

He sighed. "They searched the building again. Just outside the back door, they found something we missed—a rag that smelled of chloroform."

I felt a chill. Whoever it was had been prepared.

"It's obvious that Anna was quickly bundled into an expressman's cart and taken away. She could be anywhere by now. The police are setting watches at the local train stations in the area, as well as the bridges out of the city."

"Poor Anna."

Cullom shifted in his seat. "I still don't understand why she would be taken."

I shared my theory of the Zaleskis' involvement with the anarchist group in Chicago and my plan for how to proceed in the morning.

His frown deepened. "I will be in meetings all week. If you are off investigating, who is to stay with Claudine? I don't want to leave her safety to the staff. You agree there may still be a danger to her?"

"We must proceed on that assumption. I'll take Claudine with me."

Cullom raised a skeptical eyebrow. "To meet a bomb-maker?"

"Claudine is sturdier than you realize. After all, within the past few days an intruder was shot mere yards from her door and her best friend has gone missing. I doubt her sensibilities will be any further outraged by meeting a man who makes bombs for his livelihood."

He hesitated.

"I shall refrain from requesting a tour of his laboratory, if you wish," I added dryly.

I may have seen a ghost of a smile on Cullom's face, or perhaps it was the play of firelight. "Our lives were rather humdrum before you came to Washington, Miss Hamilton."

CHAPTER 15

MONDAY, JANUARY 17, 1887

I was up early, eager to get started. As bomb-makers are seldom found in the city directory, I was counting upon Frank to know where I could find Artie Lindquist. Cullom rose early as well, breakfasted quickly, and left, with a promise to send my telegram right away. "I'll have them deliver the response here."

Claudine came down to the dining room as I was finishing my coffee. Her eyes were red-rimmed, her face pale. "Any word on Anna?" she whispered.

"I'm sorry, dear. Nothing yet." I went over to the toast rack and got her a plate.

"I'm not hungry."

"Well, try anyway," I urged. "We have a difficult day ahead of us."

She frowned as I told her my theory as to why Anna was kidnapped. "I don't know, Pen. The Zaleskis have been nothing but kind to me. It's hard to imagine them associating with anarchists and hurting people."

"That may not be exactly what it is. Perhaps Mr. Zaleski inadvertently learned something, and now the anarchists are worried the police interrogation will bring it to light."

"What are we going to do?"

I explained my next step, and her eyes widened.

"We're going to talk to someone who makes...bombs?" she said incredulously.

"If I can find him—"

The doorbell rang. Though my heart raced of its own accord, I knew it was too soon for an answer to my telegram.

Quick footsteps approached the dining room, and there stood Phillip Kendall.

If I had realized Claudine would fling herself at the man and sob into his jacket, I would have intervened. Of course, I should have anticipated it, as I was tempted to do so myself. But it wasn't propriety that held me back from such a display. It was what I had seen last night.

I gave him a disapproving frown as he put his arms around the girl and let her cry on his lapels. He returned my look with a helpless grimace. I got up and finally managed to peel her away from him.

"I heard about Miss Zaleski," he said. "I wanted to see how I could help."

The last thing I wanted was Phillip Kendall's assistance. "Claudine, I need to speak with Mr. Kendall alone. Wait for me in the library, would you?" I passed her a clean handkerchief, and she left, still sniffling.

"Let us talk in the parlor," I murmured to Kendall.

He followed me in, and I turned to face him. "Close the door, if you please," I snapped.

"What is it, Pen? It is not just the girl's disappearance that has you upset."

He was right about that. I was angry—angry with myself. I had allowed him and his doings to distract me last night. I should have been keeping a watchful eye on Claudine and Anna. This never should have happened.

I also felt betrayed. I realized that I'd fallen for that chastened-little-boy routine at our parting last summer—the avowal of a man setting out to reform his life. Had I wanted to believe it because he was handsome and charming? I felt the flush creep up my cheeks. Well, I wouldn't be fooled again.

I clenched my fists at my sides. "You, sir, are a *thief*. I want you to stay away from me, and especially from Miss Pelley."

Kendall frowned. "What on earth are you—" He sucked in a breath. "Ah, I see."

"*You* see? I saw plenty at the Corcoran last night. I saw how you honed in on the woman in the pearl choker, then I saw your neat little trick where you helped her *into* her coat and *out* of her neck—necklace." I took a breath to steady my trembling voice. It threatened to betray me.

Kendall thrust his hands in his pockets. "I'm sorry you saw that. I can't explain, except to say that it is not what it appears."

I raised an eyebrow. "You are saying you *didn't* steal the choker?"

"I did, but—" He sighed.

I turned toward the window and groped for my handkerchief. *Drat*, I'd lent it to Claudine. Kendall came up behind me and silently passed one over my shoulder.

When I'd stopped sniffling, he took me by the arms and turned me, gently, to face him again. I looked up into his dark-brown eyes—eyes that looked so honest and trustworthy, whether they were brimming with humor, or sorrow, or compassion. But these were the eyes of a liar. Oh, how I wanted to trust him! But that would be foolhardy in the extreme. I'd seen what I'd seen.

I could not love a thief.

Love? Who was talking about love? My breath caught. Heavens, what was happening here?

His hands still gripped my arms. "Pen," he murmured, drawing me closer, "trust me. Please." And then he kissed me.

As kisses go, it was rather pleasant. For a moment, I felt as if I were a spectator in my own body, noting the lean, muscled arm that firmly cradled my neck, the tickle of his mustache against my skin, the heady taste of his lips as my mouth parted of its own volition and I kissed him back.

I abruptly broke the embrace, and my inner looker-on retreated in disappointment.

Kendall dropped his arms. "I know I'm supposed to apologize for taking liberties, but I can't say that I'm sorry." A small smile twitched his lips. "You're an attractive woman, Pen."

"And a *married* one," I retorted. A terrible, complicated situation to be in. Married, but never kissed again? It was too sad to contemplate. And to pick a thief as a lover...I drew a breath. "Is this how you cajole your reluctant paramours? Or woo rich ladies before you liberate them of their jewels?"

His brow lowered. "I wouldn't know," he responded tartly. "None of them was reluctant."

That I could believe.

"I know what you saw last night seems to lead to one conclusion," he went on. "I'm asking you to trust me. And to let me help you find Anna."

I walked to the parlor door—my vision more blurry with each step—and opened it. "Goodbye, Mr. Kendall."

I kept my face averted as he passed.

I had just collected myself and was headed to the library when the doorbell rang again. Both Hattie and Claudine rushed ahead of me to get it. The entire household was on tenterhooks, eager for word about Anna.

After a quick interchange with the stranger at the door, Hattie returned with a folded slip of paper. My heart beat faster at the sight of the telegram. Claudine read over my shoulder as I unfolded it. It was from Frank.

L. RELOCATED OPERATIONS SEVERAL YEARS AGO AFTER RECOVERING. LAST KNOWN: WHITEHALL ALLEY ACROSS FROM COAL YARD. LAST BUILDING ON LEFT, SECOND FLOOR. GOOD LUCK. MESSAGE IF YOU NEED ME.

Bless the man. Despite our differences, he was always ready to come to my aid. But I hoped to wrap this up more quickly than it would take him to get here.

I glanced at the messenger. "Thank you. There is no response." He tipped his cap and left.

Hattie waited nearby. "Anything I can do for you, miss?"

"Call a cab, if you would. Miss Claudine and I are going out." Claudine ran to fetch her coat.

Fortunately, the driver knew how to get to Whitehall Alley. This neighborhood embraced a mixture of functions, from manufacture—we noted a candy factory as we passed—to awninged storefronts of bookseller, grocer, and tobacconist, to private residences of wood clapboard. A Methodist church on the corner lent a respectable air to the whole. The driver looked askance when we had him drop us off at the coal yard. Well, the alley *was* rather narrow and dark. I couldn't say I wasn't experiencing some trepidation myself.

I handed him another bill from my reticule. "Please wait." I wasn't sure if we could get a cab easily in this neighborhood.

"All right, miss." He gestured toward the wider part of the alley, beside the coal yard fence. "I'll wait over there for ya."

Claudine was already heading down the alley. "Look, Pen— there." She pointed to a gray-painted wood door at the left end of the row. "That must be it." It was unlocked, and we stepped in. Here the building had been made into four apartment dwellings, two on each level. I ran a gloved finger over the listing of names nailed to the wall of the foyer. *A. Lindquist, #4*

As we reached the top of the stairs, I leaned in to whisper to Claudine. "I may need you to wait downstairs. I don't know if he has his operations here or elsewhere. The substances he works with are volatile."

She gave a wide-eyed nod as I knocked.

I heard the sounds of shuffling feet. Then a wheezy, male voice called, "Who's there?"

I frowned. The voice didn't sound familiar. Did he have company? "Mr. Lindquist? Is that you? It's Mrs....Wynch."

I winced as Claudine gaped at me. I'd forgotten she didn't know Frank and I were married.

"Mrs. *Wynch?*" The door opened a crack. The room beyond was dark. I couldn't see the man at all.

I leaned closer. "Yes, although I go by Miss Hamilton now. I have a friend with me. We mean you no trouble, I assure you."

The door opened a bit more, then stopped.

"May we come in?" I prompted.

"Just a moment."

More shuffling, and then he called to us from farther inside the room. "Come in."

I pushed the door open. The room was dark, except for what little light came through the window, where the shade had been drawn up a few inches. It was enough for us to maneuver around the furniture. Lindquist—if it was he—stood in the far corner of the room, away from the light. He wore a hood whose folds obscured the sides of his face. Claudine gave me an anxious glance.

He motioned for us to sit. "What brings you to my little corner of the world, Mrs. Wynch? Though you say it's now Miss Hamilton—what happened to your husband?"

It was then that I knew I was indeed talking to Artie Lindquist. The phrase *my little corner of the world* was a favorite of his. "I wasn't so sure it was you at first, Mr. Lindquist. Your voice sounds quite different."

He gave a bitter wheeze. "The fire—of course you remember, you pulled me out of it and rolled me in your cloak—damaged my lungs." He gestured toward the hood. "It wasn't kind to my face either."

I suppressed a shudder. "I am glad you survived. After the accident, did you resume your...operations?"

He turned his head to Claudine. "And who is this, please?"

"I am Claudine Pelley, grandniece of—"

I put out a hand to quiet her. "Grandniece of a friend of mine," I finished smoothly. Heaven forfend Lindquist learn Claudine was related to a member of Congress. We would be shown the door immediately. "She is in my charge. Her life may be in danger. Her best friend was kidnapped last night while we attended a function at the Corcoran Gallery. That is why we are here. So, *do* you still make bombs?"

He gave a raspy chuckle. "You always were a bit on the blunt side, Pen—may I call you that? I heard Frank address you so. It suits you."

I inclined my head. He could call me the very devil, as long as I got what I needed.

"Where is Frank, by the way? Dead?"

"No, he's very much alive. I still work with him from time to time—he's the one who told me where to find you. But we no longer...live together."

Without seeing the man's face, it was difficult to register his reaction. On the other hand, Claudine's eyes were so wide it was nearly comical. I suppressed a sigh. No doubt there would be a number of questions from that quarter.

"I see." He gave a hoarse chuckle. "Well, I always thought you could do better than Frank."

I ignored that. "You haven't answered my question."

"What a persistent woman you are. Yes, I do some odd jobs, from time to time, though as you might imagine, I no longer work with nitroglycerin."

Claudine gave a start. "You don't work from *here*, do you?"

"No, my little miss, I do not," he said tartly. "That would be rather foolhardy." He turned back to me. "What do you want to know?"

I related my theory as to why Anna might have been taken, explaining that her family was being questioned by the police regarding their suspected association with the anarchists behind the Haymarket bombing. I also detailed Lightfoot Lenny's surveillance of their house and mine in Chicago, then following us to Washington, and what we knew of his actions just before his death.

Lindquist was silent for a long while after I finished. "I heard about the Haymarket affair, of course," he said finally. He shook his head. "Hot-headed, bumbling fools. The bomb was one of Lingg's. And a rather sloppy one at that. Brittle casing. It's a wonder it didn't go off before it left his laboratory."

I wasn't interested in the incompetencies of rival bomb-makers. "Who could have kidnapped Anna? Is there an anarchist group here in Washington to whom the Chicago group would have appealed for aid?"

He shook his head. "You're thinking like a Pinkerton. They aren't that organized, especially long-distance."

I heard Claudine sigh.

I persisted. "If you were to kidnap a girl, where would you hide her?"

"You should know kidnapping children is not at all in my line," he barked.

"That's not what I meant."

He shrugged. "Old warehouses, abandoned railroad depots, empty shops, someone's basement or shed."

I shuddered, imagining a panicked young girl in such a setting.

"No doubt the police are looking in those places," he added. "Was there any sign of violence or a struggle?"

I shook my head. "They used chloroform to overcome her. The police found a rag soaked in it along with one of her gloves on the loading dock behind the gallery."

"My guess, then, is that her abductors didn't take her far," he said. "Chloroform wears off quickly. They would want to secure her somewhere right away and reduce the risk of her struggles and cries attracting attention."

I sat up straighter. "So, a block or two?"

"No more. You say it was a special event at the gallery, yes? Traffic in the area would have slowed them down."

I collected my purse and stood, as did Claudine. I may not be able to figure out the *why* or the *who* of this case until after Anna was found, but at least I had some possibilities to pursue as to the question of *where*. "Thank you."

He sighed. "It appears I shall have to move again. Give Frank my regards."

CHAPTER 16

"Now what?" Claudine asked, as we rattled off in the cab.

"We're only a few blocks from the Capitol. We should speak with your uncle. I want him to find out whether the police are working on the assumption that Anna could still be close by. Besides, he may have word of a new development."

The ride took a bit longer than anticipated. It was the noon hour, and East Capitol Street was beset with foot and carriage traffic that slowed us to a crawl. Finally, we turned onto the broad drive in front of the Capitol building.

"Which entrance do ya want?" the driver called back.

"The Senate Chamber, if you please," I said.

"Ladies' reception room, then, on the eastern side?" he asked.

"Thank you," I said.

We were grateful for his diligence, as the bracing wind whipped at us along the broad steps to the eastern entrance. At least we didn't have far to walk.

We were ushered into the space set aside for lady visitors and stated our business to the clerk.

He sucked in his cheek thoughtfully. "Mr. Cullom? Last I saw him, he was working at his desk in the chamber. I'll go check."

"Where do the stairs lead?" Claudine asked, pointing to our left.

"To the ladies' viewing gallery," he said. "You're welcome to go up and take a look, though there isn't a session going on at the moment. I'll be right back."

It was a breathtaking view of the entire chamber below, covered in a deep-hued purple carpet in a floral pattern. Well-polished mahogany desks—most piled with stacks of papers—curved in concentric rows facing a raised dais with desks for the presiding officer and others. Set into the coffered, iron ceiling were three rows of glass panels with gilded trim. The effect was light and airy, though rather drafty this time of year.

Claudine was leaning over the railing. "I don't see Uncle Shelby."

There were several men working at their desks below, but I didn't see him, either.

The clerk came huffing up the steps. "I've been told he's in the dining room. This way, ladies."

After turning down a maze of corridors, the appetizing smells of roast beef and mushroom gravy greeted us. My stomach rumbled, and I realized breakfast had been several hours ago.

The clerk approached the maître d' in the dining foyer and murmured in his ear. The man inclined his head.

"This is where I must leave you," the clerk said to us with a bow.

The maître d' led the way through the dining room. Every table was occupied, and my attention was torn between looking ahead to see where the man was going and watching my skirts so that I wouldn't catch them on anything. Despite my caution, my skirt snagged on the point of an umbrella hooked over the back of a gentleman's chair. "I beg your pardon," I murmured, stooping to un-catch my hem.

He jumped to his feet. "Allow me to help you."

Then I observed his table companions. *Oh no.* Lydia Engels and—Phillip Kendall. My heart fluttered painfully in my chest.

Kendall looked as distressed as I'm sure I did. He gave Mrs. Engels a quick glance as he got to his feet. "Miss Hamilton...you already know Lydia...allow me to present Congressman Walter Engels—"

"I'm sorry," I interrupted, feeling the heat rise up my neck, "I haven't the time. Excuse me." I gathered my skirts to catch up to Claudine. As I turned away, I noticed Lydia looking back and forth between Kendall and myself, a puzzled frown tugging at her brow.

If she only knew.

Cullom looked up in surprise as we approached, hastily brushing crumbs from his vest. "Ladies! Is there news?" He got to his feet, as did the other two gentlemen at his table, Collis Huntington and Jacob Graham. We must have interrupted another round of talks.

I shook my head. "Not of that sort. May we speak to you?"

"Please, sit down." Cullom gestured to an empty chair between him and Huntington, who held it out for me.

Claudine didn't require a second invitation and promptly plunked herself in the chair that Graham had pulled out. "Uncle Shelby, we have an idea where Anna could be."

This was *not* a conversation for other ears—especially Huntington's, if he was involved in Anna's disappearance. Lindquist had destroyed any spurious theories of anarchists I might have had, so we were back to the railroad magnate. However, I was too far away to poke the girl. I had to settle for a warning look, which she ignored.

Jacob Graham leaned forward in curiosity. "Anna—she is your friend, is that right?"

Claudine nodded.

"Something has happened to her?" He glanced at Cullom, who gave a curt nod.

"She disappeared at the art auction last night," Claudine said. "We searched the entire gallery. Someone has abducted her."

Collis Huntington frowned. "Abducted? Why would someone do such a thing?"

Cullom gave him a steady look. "We have been wondering that ourselves."

Graham glanced between Cullom and Huntington, his brow furrowed. Then it smoothed in understanding.

Red-faced, Huntington threw his napkin on the table and pushed his chair back. "It's time I should be going," he muttered.

In the silence that followed Huntington's departure, Cullom cleared his throat. "I suppose I could have handled that better. I don't *really* suspect him of being behind Miss Zaleski's disappearance."

Graham waved a dismissive hand. "He'll get over it. He has a great deal on his mind with this bill, as do you."

"It doesn't seem to bother you, sir," I observed.

Graham shrugged. "My money isn't tied up in railroad stock. No doubt it will be an inconvenience, but I'll find a way to adapt. I always do."

Cullom turned to Claudine. "You have information as to where Anna might be?"

"Not specifically," the girl said, "but Pen's friend thinks that she's somewhere near the gallery."

Jacob Graham frowned. "Friend?"

Claudine leaned forward eagerly. "There's this man—"

"Just an acquaintance," I interrupted smoothly. The less said about me being on speaking terms with a bomb-maker in front of Graham, the better.

"Why nearby?" Graham asked. "If she was taken by vehicle, she could be headed to New York by now."

I explained what we learned about the short-acting effects of chloroform and the constraints of last night's crowd. "Though she could have been moved since," I added, grimacing in Cullom's direction. "But it would be safest to move her at night. They may be waiting until then. We have very little time."

He stood. "I'll contact Captain North immediately. You ladies go home and wait. I'll send word as soon as we know something."

Claudine nodded, white-lipped. "Hurry, Uncle Shelby. Please."

Graham also stood and bowed politely. "You are a good friend, Miss Pelley," he said to Claudine. "I'm sure Miss Zaleski would appreciate everything you're doing to try to save her."

Claudine fumbled for her handkerchief as I led her out.

"I don't want to go home and *wait*," Claudine wailed as the driver bundled us in and we pulled away from the curb. "I want to look for Anna, *now!*"

I sighed. "I understand how you feel, but it wouldn't be the prudent course. We would have to search several blocks around the gallery, knock on doors, and convince private citizens to open their homes and businesses for inspection. The police have that kind of authority. We do not."

"Can't we at least *try*? We could search abandoned lots nearby —there must be some of those."

"And if we stumble upon the kidnappers, what then? There are only the two of us. No, we are going home."

Claudine folded her arms in sulky silence. I hadn't seen her mulish side since we'd first met.

Once we were home, she went straight to her room without a word. I paced the library, a few times stopping to pick up a book, only to put it down again. I understood Claudine's disquiet. I detested having to wait for someone else to conduct a search, to look for clues, to decide the next step. I finally gave up my pacing and sat in the wingback chair by the fire.

A brisk knock upon the library door lintel roused me sometime later. I must have fallen asleep. Again. Webb stepped in.

"Someone to see you, miss." He squinted at the card. "A...Mrs. Engels."

Lydia? What on earth was she doing here? "Send her in," I said, standing up and smoothing my skirt.

The woman entered, swathed in a fox fur stole, the scent of rosewater trailing in her wake. "Miss Hamilton. Thank you for seeing me."

"Of course. This is...a surprise." I looked over her shoulder. "Neither your husband nor Mr. Kendall has accompanied you here?"

"No, I wished to speak with you in private." She hesitated. "May I close the door?"

I nodded.

We sat across from each other by the fire.

Lydia removed her stole, set her purse aside, tugged at her gloves, and fussed with the folds of her skirt. Why was she so nervous?

The silence lengthened beyond my already-depleted patience. "What did you wish to talk about, Mrs. Engels?" I asked finally.

"It's about Phillip."

"Phillip."

"Yes. There has been a grievous misunderstanding. I want to clear it up."

I could feel the flush of anger suffusing my cheeks. "Did he send you?"

"No, no. He doesn't know I'm here."

I rubbed my temples. Here was an additional complication I didn't need at the moment. "What misunderstanding is that?" I asked wearily.

"You saw him take the necklace last night."

I looked over at her in surprise. "You know about that?" Good Lord, had I stumbled upon a den of jewel thieves? Was it her task to identify the valuable pieces among her social set for him to steal? It was an exercise of will to rein in my imaginings.

THE CASE OF THE RUNAWAY GIRL

"Of course I know." She reached into her purse and pulled out a framed, tintype photograph. "The pearl choker is mine, you see. Walter's wedding gift."

Sure enough, a twenty-years-younger Mrs. Walter Engels stood in a stiff pose, attired in her wedding dress, choker at her throat.

"You are saying Mr. Kendall *stole it back* for you?"

She nodded.

A wave of relief washed over me. Kendall was a thief, but *not* a thief. And yet, a number of questions remained. "Why on earth would he have to use such means to get it back? How did another woman come to be in possession of the necklace to begin—" My mouth dropped open as it hit me. *Of course.*

Mrs. Engels flushed a dusky red and looked down at her shoes.

I sat back and considered how to phrase this delicately. Some say I can be disconcertingly blunt. "Someone stole it from you," I began, "but under…compromising circumstances, is that correct? You could not go to the police."

"I could not."

"Obviously, you know who took it. A—a lover? Who then gave it to someone else?"

Another nod. Still, she didn't meet my eye.

"You confronted the man?"

She gritted her teeth. "He laughed in my face. Said it was fair *recompense*. He knew there was nothing I could do."

"Your trust in him was sadly misplaced."

She looked at me then, brow lowered, nostrils flared. "Obviously," she snapped. She took a breath. "You do not know, Miss Hamilton—as a single woman—what it is like to be married to a man who has broken your heart. Walter isn't at all the man I thought. He has a cruel temper. And he has betrayed me—more than once."

She could not know, of course, that I understood exactly how she felt. "I'm not here to judge you, Mrs. Engels," I said quietly.

She fumbled for her handkerchief. "I cannot seem to pick a good man, no matter how hard I try."

"Your situation is a difficult one," I observed. "I am glad you have your pearls back, at least. I assume your husband is unaware of what happened? You and Mr. Kendall kept it between you?"

She nodded. "Phillip has been the soul of discretion."

A prickle of jealousy made me wonder, briefly, what else Kendall and Lydia kept between them. Absurd, I know. I firmly brought my thoughts back to the business at hand. "How did Mr. Kendall discover the whereabouts of your necklace?"

"He first tried searching the house of the man who took it, without success. Then he spent a week tracking down the man's other—paramours. I had no idea there were *others*. I've been such a fool," she added bitterly.

"I see. But why have you told me this?" Not exactly a secret one unburdens to a mere acquaintance.

She grimaced. "Phillip was greatly troubled after seeing you today, and it took me a while before I could coax the story from him. I do not want my troubles to be the ruin of someone else's relationship. The two of you seem...well matched."

Now it was my turn to blush. "There is far too much upheaval in the Cullom household to concern myself with anything of *that* nature." And as long as I was still married to Frank, I could not contemplate a romantic attachment. Ever.

Her eyes softened. "Phillip can help you, you know. Has there been any word about the girl?"

I shook my head. "The senator is asking the police to again search the immediate area surrounding the Corcoran Gallery. We don't think she was taken far. At least not yet. There is the concern that she may be moved tonight."

She raised an eyebrow. "Did they thoroughly search the gallery premises? Besides the two floors open to the public, there is a basement as well."

"Yes, the basement level is a veritable maze. I remember it

being accessible only from the janitor's closet. But what makes you think the basement a likely place?"

She shrugged. "I've never been down there, but given the history of the building and all of the renovations and tear-downs, it might be worth another look."

"Oh?"

"During the war, the quartermaster took over the building to use as a uniform depot. At the time, the interior had not yet been completed. They put in floors, ceilings, and walls, dividing the space into offices and storage rooms. Once Mr. Corcoran got it back after the war, he had to rip out everything to restore the interior to museum standards."

I nodded. "It is a beautiful gallery."

"My point is, the spaces *not* open to the public—such as the basement—may not have gotten the same careful renovation," Mrs. Engels said.

"Meaning there could be sealed-off sections or some such?" I bit my lip as I thought back. We had conducted our search by lantern light, as had the police. "That's a bit of a stretch, surely? Mr. Brixton would have directed the police to all of the possible spaces to hide Anna."

"The assistant curator?" She frowned. "I suppose, though he's new. He may not know every nook and cranny."

"How is it *you* are so familiar with the gallery?"

"Walter is on the board of trustees. I suppose we could ask him..." Her brow cleared. "Your butler, Webb, knows the place. It would be more expedient to speak with him."

"Webb? Oh, that's right. The Huntingtons mentioned he'd had a studio there."

Mrs. Engels was already reaching for the bell pull.

After a couple of minutes, there was a polite knock.

"Come in!" I called.

We heard the knob rattle. "It's Hattie, miss. Can you unlock the door?"

I frowned at Mrs. Engels, who shrugged. "I didn't lock it."

I went over to the door. There was no key in it, but it was certainly locked fast. "Get Mrs. Webb to come with the key, Hattie. Oh, and tell her husband that we want to talk to him."

"Yes, miss." We heard her footsteps hurrying down the corridor.

"This is decidedly odd," I said. "Doors do not lock themselves."

I paced the room while we waited. After what seemed a long interval, the girl returned. "I can't find 'em anywhere, miss," she called.

"*Neither* one?" I searched my memory to think whether either of them had mentioned an outing or errand. I shook my head. I had not been here much of the day.

"What should I do now?" Hattie asked.

"Fetch Miss Claudine. The two of you can look for Mrs. Webb's keys." I hoped the woman hadn't taken them with her. Where could she be? And her husband, too? A prickle of unease plucked at my spine.

I looked over at Mrs. Engels, sitting quietly and contemplating the fire. "I am sorry for the inconvenience. What a ludicrous situation."

She gave a wan smile. "It's all right. I'm in no hurry."

Hattie returned on running feet. "Miss Hamilton?" Her voice was edged in panic. "Miss Claudine, she's—she's *gone.*"

CHAPTER 17

I ran to the parlor window to look out on the darkening street. No sign of Claudine or the Webbs. No conveyance lingered outside. How long had they been gone? Had the three of them left together? I had a bad feeling about this.

"Surely you are not contemplating climbing out of the window," Mrs. Engels said.

I shook my head, looking down at the ten-foot drop to the concrete below. Each of the rowhomes along this stretch had elevated front entrances, and the steps were well out of reach of the window. "Is your carriage nearby?"

She came to the window and pointed across the park. "I asked the driver to wait on the far side of the circle until he saw me come out."

"May we use it?"

"Of course."

I went over to the door, reaching into my chignon for a hairpin.

"Hattie?" I called through the door as I put the pin in the lock. "Are you still there?"

"Yes, miss."

"Did you see Miss Claudine leave?"

"No. But she's not in the house. I looked everywhere. I even asked the other maid, Gertie. She's the only other one here in the house right now besides the cook, who wants to know when to serve dinner."

I checked the time. *Mercy*, five thirty already. "Hattie, you're sure that Miss Claudine said nothing to either of you about going out?"

"I'm sure."

"Did she leave a note?"

"No, miss." Her voice sounded miserable now.

I wiggled the hairpin in the hole, trying to get at the mechanism. "All right, Hattie. I'm working on the lock from this side. In the meantime, I want you to go across the park where Mrs. Engels's carriage is waiting. That's the lady who's locked in here with me." I turned aside to her. "What's your driver's name?"

"Benjamin."

I turned back to the door. "Did you hear that, Hattie? The driver's name is Benjamin. Tell him who you are and that Mrs. Engels wants him to drive you to see Senator Cullom at the Capitol—"

"Oh, miss!" Hattie interrupted in alarm. "They'd never let the likes of me in the door!"

I grimaced. She had a point. A little colored girl trying to get into the Senate Chamber to talk to Senator Cullom? "I'll write you a note to show them. Hold on."

I left the pin hanging out of the lock and went to the writing desk.

Senator,

Please come home immediately. Claudine is missing. Webbs are gone, too.

~Penelope Hamilton

I folded it and slipped it under the door. "Show them that."

"But, miss…" Her voice trailed off.

"It's for Claudine's sake. You can do this, Hattie. You are a brave young lady."

I heard her expel a breath. "All right. I'll go."

"Good girl. *Hurry.*"

Mrs. Engels went to the window to watch. I resumed my work on the lock, all the while considering the possibilities. Webb had deliberately locked us in, I was sure of it. He'd escorted Mrs. Engels in here, watched her close the door behind her, and simply turned the key and took it. An effective tactic. It hampered my ability to follow them, should I notice them leave.

But I had been too distracted to notice—by the affairs of Phillip Kendall. Again.

Even so, I was sure to have heard them if Claudine had been taken by force. How had they convinced her to accompany them willingly? Had they concocted a story, perhaps a spurious message from Anna? Or did they use chloroform on her as well? Their conveyance would have had to be nearby. Perhaps parked around the corner out of sight on Rhode Island Avenue. Then it would be a simple matter of a few steps out the back door and through the gate.

I had been suspicious of the Webbs when they'd first arrived, but eventually had come to accept that they were what they seemed to be. What had finally convinced me? Then I remembered. Webb had shot and killed Lightfoot Lenny. He wouldn't do that if they were working together.

Or would he? Webb had known the senator was closing in on Leonard Crill. Had he tried to warn off his accomplice and failed? I recalled, during the night, the sound of the back door slamming, Mrs. Webb's low murmur. Had a warning message been sent to Crill?

Or perhaps Webb had sent a message to the man in charge of it all—Huntington—with a request for instructions. Had Webb been told to kill Lightfoot Lenny before he could be captured and reveal what he knew?

I'd been struck by how Lightfoot Lenny was surprised at being shot by Webb. *Not the plan*, he'd gasped in his dying moment. But there had been something else...what was it? I shut my eyes briefly to concentrate. *Why did he...? Webb...*

How did he know Webb's name? The Webbs were hired after Crill had stopped watching the house. But if they were working for the same man...no wonder he'd been surprised to be shot by a confederate.

The pin stuck, and I had to wrench it out.

I heard Mrs. Engels sigh. "It's hard to tell by the streetlamps in the distance, but Benjamin seems to be arguing with the girl. The coach hasn't moved. How is the lock coming along?"

"I've bent this hairpin beyond its usefulness," I said ruefully, setting it aside and groping in my hair for another.

She came over to watch. "How on earth do you know how to pick a lock?"

"Didn't Mr. Kendall tell you?" I mumbled, pin in my mouth as I repositioned the others to keep the hair out of my eyes. "I'm a Pinkerton."

"How interesting! No, he never said anything about that." She turned back to the window. "Ah, it looks as if she has convinced him at last. They are climbing in."

Good girl. I blew out a breath and bent over the keyhole with the fresh pin. What I wouldn't give for my lockpicks right now.

The second one finally got the door open. Even the ever-patient Lydia Engels looked relieved.

"Shall I have Gertie call you a cab, Mrs. Engels?" I asked. "I don't know when Hattie and your driver will be back."

She shook her head. "I'll stay. And please, call me Lydia. I want to help. What can I do?"

I gave her an assessing look. She seemed perfectly sincere, and we could use another ally right now. "Well, then, I think we should—" I broke off at the sound of the doorbell.

I was too impatient to wait for Gertie and yanked it open.

THE CASE OF THE RUNAWAY GIRL

"Mrs. Kroger? What on earth are you doing here? Aren't you supposed to be in Boston?"

The housekeeper, valise in one hand and cane in the other, glared at me. "It was a fool's errand. My sister never sent for me. Just wait until I catch the prankster."

I reached for her case. It was more than a prank. It was clear, now, that the Webbs had wanted her out of the way for these few days.

Aggrieved tirade done, she finally seemed to take stock of her surroundings. "Why are *you* answering the door? Where's that laggard, Webb?"

"It's a long story," I said wearily.

As Lydia helped Mrs. Kroger through the door and onto the foyer bench, I caught up the housekeeper as succinctly as I could.

I cut across the woman's exclamations, which rose in volume when she learned that Hattie had been sent to fetch the senator. The housekeeper was surprisingly protective of the girl. "I'm sorry, Mrs. Kroger, we have no time. Mrs. Engels and I must search the rooms of those who are missing." I turned to Lydia. "Check Claudine's room, in case there is a clue as to where she has gone. I'll search the Webbs'. No doubt they have packed up and fled, but there may be something."

"All right. Which is Claudine's?" Lydia asked.

"Up the stairs, second door on your left," Mrs. Kroger said, hoisting herself up with her cane. "I'll help you look."

As soon as I entered the bedroom the Webbs shared, I knew they had indeed abandoned the Cullom house for good. Drawers had been left open and were bare of clothes, toiletries, and other personal effects. The armoire was equally empty. I scoured the room nevertheless, looking under the beds and behind furniture, in search of any object or scrap of paper that could give me a clue as to where they took Claudine.

I found one item of interest, a newspaper clipping crumpled

up in the waste basket. I brought it over to the lamp and smoothed it out. It was from yesterday's *Evening Star*.

Mr. Graham Named to Top Railroad Position

Collis P. Huntington, *major railroad developer and owner of several lines, including our local Chesapeake and Ohio Railway, has named the young, up-and-coming industrialist Jacob Graham to the position of Chief Operations Officer of the C&O Railway, effective immediately.*

I skimmed the rest of the article, which detailed Graham's background and qualifications and the sudden ouster of the former operations officer. Graham was credited with exposing an attempt by the former officer to form a cadre of rival owners to buy up Huntington's shares and take over the C&O. That investigation was pending.

I shook my head. This wasn't making sense. Why would Webb be interested in such a notice?

Lydia stood in the doorway. "Mrs. Kroger is searching the library now. But we found something in Claudine's room." She held out a plain envelope. Inside was a ringlet of pale, blonde hair.

"It looks like Anna's." I swallowed. "You didn't find a note?"

Lydia shook her head. "Perhaps they took it with them."

I took a shuddering breath and sat abruptly on the bed. "Why didn't Claudine come to me before leaving?"

Lydia sat and put an arm around my shoulders. "You mustn't blame yourself. If there was a letter, it could have threatened her friend with harm unless she came alone."

"I'm sure Webb was persuasive as well," I said tartly. "That man has much to answer for." I checked my watch. Seven o'clock. "What is keeping Hattie? It has been over an hour now."

"Perhaps the senator isn't there, or they made her wait until he was finished with a meeting," Lydia said. "Despite your note, they may not have taken the girl seriously."

I stood. "I want another look inside the Corcoran Gallery. If your theory about a hidden cache is correct, Anna may have been there all along."

"Are you seriously considering going there *now?*" she asked. "Should we not wait until Mr. Cullom arrives?"

I wondered if my lockpicks would be equal to whatever the gallery had installed to protect artwork worth a fortune. Probably not. What about Phillip Kendall's lockpicks? Possibly. But there was no time to get them.

"Miss Hamilton?" Lydia persisted.

"*Hmm?* Oh, sorry. No, I cannot wait any longer. It may already be too late."

"Too late? Oh, you mean the girls may have been moved by now."

"Actually, I believe the Webbs have Claudine with them and plan to retrieve Anna once the staff has gone for the night and the roads are less trafficked."

"And Anna was the bait all along, to get Claudine?" Lydia asked.

"It would seem so." I grimaced. The abductors—more than one was needed, I was certain, in order to accomplish Anna's capture at a crowded gallery event—had proved eminently adaptable. I had no doubt they'd originally intended to kidnap Claudine during the art auction, but when no opportunity presented itself, they had looked to Anna. Grab Anna, stash her nearby, but drop her glove out on the loading dock in the event of a search, as if she'd been taken out of the gallery. The chloroform rag as well. Perhaps they had planned to get a message to Claudine. Her friend was ill—come quickly. Something of the sort. Webb would have assumed the role of messenger. Claudine trusted the butler, who shouldn't have been at the gallery in the first place, I realized. But because the original driver had shown up drunk—perhaps that, too, had been a contrivance—Webb was recruited to drive the carriage and wait nearby.

But that plan hadn't worked out, either. Claudine had noticed Anna missing too soon and sought me out in the cloakroom before Webb could lure her away. They had needed to change things once again, waiting until today to get Claudine. But doing so had finally blown the Webbs' cover, and they had fled.

"Miss Hamilton!" Mrs. Kroger called from the first floor. Her voice sounded frantic.

I stuck the clipping in my pocket and hurried down the stairs, Lydia at my heels. Mrs. Kroger stood outside the door to the library, a plain white envelope in her hand, the words *Senator Cullom* sprawled across the front. "I found it on the writing desk."

I lifted the flap and pulled out the single sheet, folded around another blonde ringlet.

Senator,

If you want the young ladies returned safely, you will say you have been called away on a family emergency. Do not bring in the police. Join your wife and daughters in Charlottesville. Miss Pelley and Miss Zaleski will be returned to you there.

I showed it to Lydia.

She sucked in a breath. "Why do they want him to go to Charlottesville?"

"They know the rest of his family is there, and they want him away from the senate proceedings. Cullom has been the driving force behind the railroad bill, which is still being hotly debated and is at risk of being delayed in its passage. Should the senator bow out, it could all collapse."

"Do you know who is behind this?"

"Mr. Cullom believes it to be Collis Huntington." I had thought so, too, but after finding the clipping in the Webbs' room, another idea was forming. I wasn't sure about the entirety of it yet.

Lydia's eyes widened. "The railroad magnate? Wouldn't suspicion turn to him right away? How can he hope to get away with this?"

"I don't know. That's his problem. Right now, I have to find the girls."

"What can I do?" she asked.

I frowned. "Are you sure you want to become involved further? It's a sordid business."

Lydia shrugged. "I can look out for myself."

Mrs. Kroger took a step closer. "I want to help, too. Those good-for-nothing Webbs are going to pay!"

It was gratifying to have the dour housekeeper on my side for a change. "All right, then. Mrs. Kroger, hail a cab for Mrs. Engels. She's going to the National Hotel to fetch a friend of ours who is…good in an emergency. In the meantime, we'll need you to wait here for the senator and Hattie to return. Show Mr. Cullom the ransom note. Tell him that I'm at the Corcoran Gallery, but he must exercise caution and not rush in there openly. I don't know what we will find."

Mrs. Kroger hastened out the front door to flag down a hansom.

I turned to Lydia. "Ask Mr. Kendall to bring his lockpicks to the gallery. Tell him to make sure his vehicle stays out of sight when he approaches the building. I'll be in the back, near the loading dock. I'm going to try to get in on my own in the meantime."

She bit her lip and looked me up and down. "I hate to think of you going alone. Do be careful."

"I intend to."

CHAPTER 18

*C*fter one last check of my lockpicks and loaded gun—
secreted in my deep coat pockets—I walked the block to
Fourteenth and Rhode Island. Within minutes, a streetcar glided
to a stop, and I hopped aboard.

I decided to step off at Sixteenth and Lafayette, a block short
of the back of the gallery. The cold January evening stung my
cheeks and penetrated my gloves. I shoved my hands in my
pockets and walked briskly, my heels ringing on the pavement.
There wasn't much foot traffic on such a night, but there were still
a few people about. I waited until no one was in view to slip along
the shadows of the adjacent building and approach the loading
dock and the barred back door of the gallery.

I'd hardly opened my lockpicks case before the sound of
carriage wheels approaching sent me scurrying for a stack of
wood boxes piled beside the dock. I crouched low, not daring to
peek as I tried to listen over the sound of the racing pulse in
my ears.

I heard a carriage door opening and a pair—no, two pairs—of
footsteps, one with a heavier tread than the other. They were
approaching the back door.

"Light the lantern, you idiot. I can't see a thing!" a voice growled.

I managed to smother my near-exclamation just in time. *Jack Porter.*

He had *not* been killed by Lightfoot Lenny. He must have been working with him all along.

Jack had played his part of the jovial ally quite convincingly, even pretending to elude Crill on our way to the department store. But his annoyance had broken through that happy-go-lucky facade. It is difficult to maintain a calm demeanor when dealing with a sloppy co-conspirator who'd nearly flushed their prey. I could see it now.

But why had Crill trailed us that day? Surely Jack would have told him where we were going. He'd known where to wait later, to try to take me by force. Had he not trusted Jack and wanted to be sure?

I was so preoccupied I nearly missed the reply of the other man.

"—order me around." It was Webb's voice, no longer smooth and unctuous—more of a plaintive whine. "I've had the harder job of it, you know, running Cullom's household these last few days, putting on dinners, bowing and scraping. All you've had to do is watch the girl and keep out of sight. This had better be worth it. I don't know if he's really going to pay us what he says. It's a lot of money."

"Quit yer whining," Jack retorted. "He'll pay."

I heard the scrape of a bolt shot back and waited until their voices faded inside before running to the carriage. It was Jack's, all right—I recognized the smudge of pale paint on the fender. The curtains over the windows were drawn. I went over to the left side door, farthest from view of the back door, and eased it open.

Inside lay Claudine, eyes closed. I whipped off the blanket covering her. Her wrists and ankles were bound with rough cord.

I shook her. "Claudine!" I hissed. "Wake up!"

Her eyes fluttered. She groaned. "Pen..."

"*Shhh*, not so loudly. They may come out any minute." I was already working on the knots at her wrists, but in the dark interior I had to go by touch, and my fingers were stiff and clumsy in the cold.

"I feel so...so dizzy."

"I know. I'm working on your bindings now, and we'll get you out into the fresh air." I tried to sound more confident than I felt. I doubted she could walk right away, and I wasn't sure I could carry her, even as petite as she was. And what about Anna?

I blew out a breath. One girl at a time.

Claudine's eyes were drifting closed.

"How did they lure you to the carriage?" I whispered, trying to keep her awake.

"Mrs. Webb...gave me a note," she mumbled. "It had Anna's— Anna's hair inside."

I was down to the last knot under her hands, and my eyes were adjusting to the dark. "Why didn't you come tell me?"

A sliver of moonlight coming through a gap in the curtains showed the gleam of tears upon her cheeks. "I was still angry at you...not looking for her. I showed Mrs. Webb the note. She said you'd stepped out. She promised to go with me...stop at the police station on the way...get help."

"What happened then?"

"We got to the carriage...I recognized it."

"Jack's carriage," I said.

She swallowed, her eyes open now, more fully awake. "Yes. That bit of paint on the fender. But before I could ask, Webb walked up. He pushed a cloth in my face. It happened so fast."

I nodded. The last knot at her wrists was coming out now. "Chloroform. What then? Did you wake up at any point after that?"

"A few times, then I'd fall asleep again. I couldn't summon the energy to try to get out of my bindings the way you taught me."

She sighed. "I've been so stupid. I'm sorry, Pen. You must be quite angry with me."

"Not at all," I soothed. "All right, your hands are free. Can you sit up while I untie—" I broke off at the sound of men's voices. "Lay back down," I whispered. "Keep your eyes closed." She stretched out, and I quickly settled the blanket over her and hid the rope beneath the seat. Her ankles were still bound, but she might be able to untie the knots herself when her captors weren't looking.

I slipped out of the carriage to resume my spot behind the crates. I pulled out my gun as I peered between the boxes, watching the two men as they emerged with a bound, inert form slung over Webb's shoulder. It was hard to see in the dim light of the lantern Jack carried, but it had to be Anna. I carefully pushed the barrel between the crates and tried to get a clear shot. Impossible—they were standing too close together. I might hit the girl, and I couldn't very well strike both men simultaneously. The other one might do something desperate and harm both young ladies. I reluctantly returned the gun to my pocket.

By the lantern light, I had a better look at Jack. He looked very much his usual, cheerful self, toothpick clenched in his teeth, grimy cap upon his red hair. I recalled the sleepless nights I'd endured when I had feared he was dead, and the depth of my anger nearly took my breath away. Cullom and I had trusted him. That had obviously worked in the abductors' favor.

And Mrs. Webb? Where was she?

The men deposited Anna in the carriage, closed the doors, and climbed onto the driver's bench in front. Claudine's pretense of unconsciousness must have succeeded. How I wished for a conveyance of my own to follow. I would have to improvise. I hunched low, scurried to the coach's running board in the back, and stepped on gingerly. I prayed they wouldn't feel the shift in weight. Apparently not. The vehicle lurched forward almost immediately.

By the time we had gained the street and were rattling along Seventeenth, I'd realized the drawbacks to my plan. I had no idea where we were going or how long it would take us to get there. Should there be other drivers along our route, someone was sure to note the ridiculous sight of a grown woman clinging to the back of a carriage in the dead of winter and alert Webb and Porter. My hands were already cramping from the cold and the exertion of maintaining my perch as the coach picked up speed. But I couldn't let go. I couldn't lose sight of the girls. If I did, I might never see them alive again.

We turned onto Pennsylvania Avenue. I turned my head just in time to see a very startled Phillip Kendall stick his head out of a carriage door and stare at me, open-mouthed. He got out, jumped up on the seat next to the driver, and grabbed the reins. Their carriage swung away from the curb in pursuit of ours.

As we slowed to pull around an expressman's wagon, I briefly freed a hand to tap on the back window. Was Claudine still conscious? To my immense relief, the curtain twitched, and the girl pressed her face to the window, her eyes widened. I put a finger to my lips before quickly re-grabbing the handle with my second hand as the coach picked up speed. I no longer had the luxury of a one-handed grip.

Claudine held a length of rope up to the window. Good girl— she must have gotten her ankles untied. I smiled, and she smiled back. Then the carriage made a sharp turn, and she disappeared from sight. Probably flung out of her seat, poor thing. Anna must already be on the floor at this rate. It was all I could do to hang on. At one point, my feet briefly left their perch.

Needless to say, I got my fair share of startled looks from those in the few vehicles we passed. No one had time to give me away, however, before our vehicle rushed past. Even so, I consider it a nine days' wonder. Soon we were turning down deserted, narrow side streets where the going was slower.

Kendall's carriage kept its distance now. I could barely see it.

He had no doubt realized the prudent course was to avoid alerting the abductors to his pursuit.

We had made so many turns that I'd lost track of where we were. At one point, we crossed a creek. This section seemed more countrified. Jack navigated more carefully along the bumpy, dark roads. Finally, we stopped in front of a white-clapboard Victorian at the end of a cul-de-sac. The streetlamps here were few and far between, the nearest one at the intersection at the top of the hill. Legs shaking, I slid off my perch and managed to duck behind a row of arborvitae near the driveway, just before the men climbed down.

I sensed movement to my right and heard the soft rustle of fabric. Phillip Kendall was skirting the shrubbery edge. We exchanged a glance as he crouched beside me, but daren't risk speaking, even in whispers.

I felt my spirits lift a little. Perhaps our odds of getting out of this mess had improved.

The front door opened. I squinted in the dim moonlight for a look at the gentleman coming briskly down the steps. I knew now who I was expecting, and it wasn't Collis P. Huntington. Jacob Graham was the one we were after.

The man was narrow-shouldered, of middling height, not easily identifiable at first—until I noted his gait. He walked as if he were springing on his toes. It was indeed Graham.

"Let's make this quick," he hissed.

Beside me, Kendall drew in a soft breath.

I understood his surprise. This was the businessman who had professed little concern for the Interstate Commerce Act, claiming to be absorbed only in his shipyard operations. Once I'd seen the newspaper notice of his new position, it was of course obvious that he had more at stake than anyone had realized. Up until a few hours ago, I'd been so sure it was Huntington.

I bit my lip. Maybe that was the point. What would happen if the blame for the kidnappings fell upon Huntington?

I set aside that question for later. At the moment, I was debating whether Kendall and I should try to overpower the three men while we were all still here in the driveway. We were outnumbered, and I was the only one of us armed, but the noise might rouse the neighbors to come to our aid. Did Webb or Porter have a gun? I hadn't seen one. But I hadn't a clue about Graham's staff inside the house.

The prudent course would be to wait. Kendall and I could reconnoiter the grounds and find an unobtrusive way into the house once it had settled down for the night. I watched as Graham strode toward Jack's carriage, wrenched open the door, and stuck his head in.

That was when Miss Claudine Pelley, with a garbled yell of fury, launched all of her ninety pounds at the man, knocking him flat on the ground. She must have untied Anna during the ride, as that young lady leapt out the opposite side, tackling Webb, who had opened the other door.

So much for the prudent course.

Not even sparing a glance at Kendall—I assumed he would follow—I pulled the gun from my pocket and ran.

CHAPTER 19

$\mathcal{A}$s rescues go, it might have had a chance. Kendall and I had the benefit of surprise, and Jack took a few steps back from Webb and Anna when I pointed the gun at him.

Kendall helped Anna up, then pushed Webb toward Jack. "Hands up. Don't move."

But Jacob Graham had gotten the advantage of Claudine. She was pinned under him on the ground now, gasping for breath.

"Graham!" I ran over to them, holding the derringer in both hands, steady at his head. "I will shoot you if necessary. Let her go. It's over."

"Not quite." A woman's voice, cold and flat, was followed by the sound of a shotgun bolt being pulled back. I turned to see Mrs. Webb striding toward us, pointing the barrel straight at Claudine. "Drop your weapon, Miss Hamilton."

I had no choice but to comply. We were quickly herded inside, and in the light of the foyer, Graham rounded upon Kendall and me. "Where did you two come from? Where is your conveyance? Did you bring others?"

Kendall and I exchanged a glance. Better to keep him guessing.

"Answer me," he snarled, leaning in close to my face and raising his palm.

Kendall stepped in to intervene, and Jack struck him on the head with his cudgel. I propped Kendall as he sagged. "Leave him alone," I snapped at Jack. "Haven't you done enough?"

The driver shrugged. "Nothin' personal, miss. Mr. Graham pays a lot better than the senator, that's all."

"And here I was worried you'd been killed," I said.

Jack curled one hand around a well-worn jacket lapel and chuckled. "I can take care of me'self. Never worry 'bout that."

"Enough!" Graham barked. "Where's your coach? How did you find us? Did you follow these buffoons?"

"It was a cab, and we dismissed it," I lied. "Besides, what does it matter? You have us now. More hostages than you anticipated, Mr. Graham. Are you going to send another ransom note to Senator Cullom?"

Graham's eyes narrowed, but he ignored the jibe. "Lock them in the basement," he said to Webb and Porter, "then search the nearby streets for their vehicle. She might be lying." He glared in my direction. "I have to consider a change in plans. The police may have been alerted."

With Porter at our backs, we followed Mrs. Webb down the narrow wood steps to a below-ground basement. The door was secured with an old, rusted padlock. She pulled it off and swung the door open. "Don't even think of yelling for help. The dirt walls are thick, and there is no neighbor close enough to hear you."

We were shoved through, down more steps. I heard the scrape of the padlock hasp snapped into place.

The space was pitch black, except for a patch of moonlight coming through a small, iron-barred transom window set high at the top of the back wall. As moths to a candle, we all headed toward that corner of the room.

"Boost me up, will you?" I said to Kendall. He lifted me by the waist and held on as I swung open the pane, testing the grate beyond.

"Anything loose?" he asked.

"I'm afraid not. And there isn't enough of a gap in the bars for someone to slip through, not even Claudine."

He set me down.

"What do we do now, Miss Hamilton?" Anna asked. The girl's voice was strained with fear and fatigue. Fortunately, I detected no hysteria there. A wonder, given all she'd endured.

"Mr. Kendall and I will come up with something." I gave Anna a hug. "Are you hurt?"

She shook her head, but I could see the gleam of tears welling up in her eyes.

I held her away from me, looking her over as my eyes adjusted to the dimness. I could make out a bruise on her left temple and raw rope burns on her wrists. Her once-lovely aquamarine silk gown was torn and soiled beyond redemption. Her blonde hair— dirty and matted—was blunt-cut, the ringlets gone. Only two curls had shown up in envelopes at Cullom's house. I wondered where the others had gotten to, but didn't speculate aloud.

"You are a brave girl," I said instead, passing her a kerchief to dab her eyes. "That was an impressive tackle. And you as well, Miss Pelley," I added, turning to Claudine, who looked in considerably better condition than her friend. "You are unharmed, I trust?"

Claudine sighed. "A bit bruised is all. But we seem to be worse off now than we were before."

There was no denying that.

Kendall had dragged over a wood crate and upended it. "You ladies sit here. Catch your breath. Miss Hamilton and I have some things to figure out."

"I want a look at you," I said to Kendall, leading him closer to the stripes of moonlight. I felt him flinch as I gently pressed the lump already forming near the back of his head. "Your scalp is bleeding. No sign of a fracture. That's something." I gathered up my skirts, fumbling for my slip in the dimness.

He laughed when he heard a *rip*. "I'm sorry you have to sacrifice your attire for my sake, Pen." He dropped his voice. "I hope this means we are friends again."

I couldn't count many people in this world who would do for me what Kendall had done. *Friends* didn't quite describe it. I kept clear of sentimental territory, however. "Of course we are friends," I said lightly. "I don't rip my second-best slip for just anyone, you know."

He grinned. "I am honored."

I folded the strip of cloth and pressed it to the wound. "This is fairly clean. Hold it here. The bleeding should stop in a few minutes."

We sat against the wall near the girls.

"Will they find your coach nearby?" I asked. Then I was struck by an alarming thought. "Lydia didn't come with you, did she?" The last thing we needed was another hostage at Graham's mercy.

"She did, but don't worry. Once we saw which house your vehicle was heading for, we pulled out of sight, and I hopped off. She and the driver have gone for the police. And Senator Cullom, too, if there's time."

"Good thinking, especially since Lydia and your driver are the only other people to know where we are now. I'm not clear myself as to our whereabouts." Clinging to the back of a moving carriage did not afford much leisure to get one's bearings.

"The cross street said Thirtieth. I didn't see a sign for this little end street. Lydia said there's a cemetery near here."

I suppressed a shudder. "Have we left the city? The houses are bigger here, spaced farther apart."

"We're just on the west edge. It was a wonder you could hold on for the entire ride." He frowned. "I was terribly worried about you." His voice grew husky.

"Never fear," I answered quickly, wishing to avoid avowals of devotion. "I have no plans to continue such antics. What time is it?"

Kendall squinted at his pocket watch. "Ten thirty."

I started. "Heavens, it's been hours. I hope she returns with the police soon. What did she tell you about all this?"

"Quite a lot." Kendall recounted the whole, omitting the original reason for the lady's visit. That remained an unspoken topic for another time, assuming we got out of this predicament and had the leisure to air it out.

"Do I have the whole story?" he asked finally, dropping his voice to a whisper. Claudine and Anna had fallen asleep, propped against each other in the corner of the wall.

"I'd say so." I pulled out the clipping I'd found in the Webbs' bedroom. "I wasn't sure what to make of this at first, but now that we're sure Jacob Graham is behind the scheme, it makes sense."

He squinted over it. "I'm afraid I can't read it in this light. What does it say?"

I gave him a quick summary. Kendall nodded. "The man seems the wide awake and ambitious sort, doesn't he?"

"I'm wondering if the takeover attempt ascribed to the former operations officer was actually a scheme of Graham's that was close to coming to light. Graham then set up the other to take the blame."

"Possible."

"I don't believe he will stop going after Huntington's holdings. What better way to distract Huntington than a kidnapping charge?"

"Still, it's a daring move on Graham's part and fraught with risk."

At that moment, we heard a heavy tread. The key turn in the padlock, and the door was opened. It was Webb, shining a lantern along the steps. "Mr. Graham wishes to see you now, Miss Hamilton." His deep, formal voice sounded absurdly as if he were announcing dinner at the Cullom house.

I got up and dusted off my skirts. Kendall made a move to follow, but Webb shook his head. "Only the lady."

I climbed the stairs, glancing back briefly at Kendall's face, pale and drawn, before Webb prodded me onward.

Jacob Graham received me in the parlor, a comfortable room I was in no position to fully appreciate. Compared to the chill, dank basement, any room would be an improvement. My pulse was racing, my abdomen clenched around the cold anger that had settled within it like a stone. I recall only a few details—the welcome warmth of the bright fire in the hearth, the creaking of the chair as I perched upon its edge, and most of all, the sight of my double-barrel derringer resting on the mahogany side table by Graham's elbow. It was tantalizingly just out of my reach.

The man himself seemed remarkably at his ease, legs crossed, puffing upon a pipe. "Well now, Miss Hamilton. Jack has been unable to find any vehicle you may have arrived in. He swears that he was not followed. How, then, did you and Mr. Kendall come to be here? And—more importantly—did you alert the police?"

"I have no obligation to tell you anything whatsoever," I retorted. "You, sir, are despicable."

He shrugged. "No matter. I'm making other arrangements."

"What arrangements are those? Moving us to yet another location? The police will catch up to you eventually."

"You do not give me enough credit. But as a woman"—he waved his pipe dismissively in my direction—"you could not possibly appreciate the scope of my plan."

"Try me."

"'I have no obligation to tell you anything whatsoever.'" He threw my words back at me.

I quirked an eyebrow. "But you are dying to tell me, are you not?" I guessed that the man's ego was warring with his caution right now. Why else would he have brought me up here?

I waited. His eyes narrowed in a wary look, but he said nothing.

"You've been quite clever," I said finally. "You had me fooled. I didn't realize until after I searched the Webbs' bedroom that you were the one behind the kidnappings and threats. I imagined it had to be someone who cared about whether or not the bill passed, and you were quite careful to demonstrate that it didn't matter so much to you. But your true goal was to discredit Collis P. Huntington, or at least distract him enough in the process of defending himself from a kidnapping charge. You set him up well. He was already an outspoken opponent of the bill, was currently residing in town, and was familiar enough with the senator's family to know that Cullom is close to his grandniece."

As was Beatrice Graham, and therefore her husband. I recalled the lady asking the girl about her Christmas scarf. I would like to think Mrs. Graham had an unwitting part to play in all this, rather than an active one.

"None of which is damning evidence against Collis," Graham mocked.

"Ah, but you also had Huntington recommend the Webbs to the senator."

He leaned back and hooked his thumbs in the armholes of his vest. "That is quite a tale. Why would I wish to discredit Collis? He is a friend and colleague of mine."

He was toying with me, but the longer I could keep him talking and possibly delay his arrangements, the better. "There is no 'friendship' in business, particularly with a man like Huntington. He saw you as a subordinate, neither a friend nor a threat. But, if he were too busy defending a kidnapping charge, you could work with his rivals to take over some of his holdings." I pulled out the newspaper clipping. "I found this in Webb's room. It's from yesterday's *Evening Star*."

Jacob Graham's eyelids flickered briefly in recognition.

"It announces your new appointment as chief operations officer of the C&O Railroad. Did you give it to Webb?"

"What if I did?" he said defensively.

I thought back to Webb's comment to Jack tonight, when they were retrieving Anna from the gallery. *I don't know if he's really going to pay us what he says.*

"Webb hasn't been entirely confident of your scheme, has he? You gave him this clipping to prove that your plan really could work, that Huntington has placed you in a position of trust and power. From there, you could gain the upper hand over Huntington."

He grunted. "The man's usually shrewder in his business dealings. This bill has set him back on his heels, and he has been relying upon me more than he normally would."

"And then you discredited the officer that Huntington had formerly trusted, shifting the blame for a takeover scheme that was really your own."

He set aside his pipe and gave me a frank appraisal. "You understand far more of the matter than I would have expected."

"Impressive for a mere woman," I retorted.

His gaze flicked over to the gun. "This is yours, is it not? When Leonard Crill told me you were a Pinkerton, I didn't believe him."

"Had you already decided by then to have Webb kill him?"

"Crill was becoming a liability—giving in to flamboyant gestures that showed his hand, failing to capture you in front of the store..." He shook his head. "In Chicago, it seemed an ideal arrangement. He owed me a favor. The plan was for him to keep an eye on Miss Pelley at the school until I was ready to act. But then the girl ran away."

"And Crill continued to follow her, even taking the train to Washington," I said.

Graham nodded. "I must admit, his tenacity was impressive. I didn't plan to kill him originally. In fact, that night I was giving him one more chance to kidnap Miss Pelley, before I paid him a nominal fee for his time and let him go."

"But Mrs. Webb got a message to you, didn't she? Was she asking for instructions, because the senator had laid a trap to catch Leonard Crill?"

He grimaced. "There was no time to get word to him, and I certainly didn't want him giving us away to Cullom when he was caught. He would ruin everything. It seemed the safest course. I knew Webb could make it look like an accident."

I shuddered at how casually Graham regarded the lives of others. It certainly did not bode well for his captives. I held little hope that he would simply let us go, although if I could convince him that the girls knew nothing...

"I didn't really need him once I had the Webbs established in Cullom's household," he added. "But I have to admit, Crill served his purpose in Chicago and *en route* here."

I guessed that was as close to a eulogy as Lightfoot Lenny was going to get.

"Where did you have Anna hidden? The police searched the entire gallery, as did we."

"Webb told me about a closed-off space in the basement, beneath one of the steam pipes," Graham said. "Used to be part of the records room during the war. A lower panel had come loose that the men pried off for access and then covered again. It was small, but adequate, until the girl could be moved tonight."

I firmly pushed aside thoughts of Anna held captive in such an airless space. It was time to focus on the present and how we were to get out of this pickle. "What are you going to do with us? You should know that Senator Cullom will never accede to your demands."

"Naturally. But as you pointed out, that was never my aim. As to what I am doing with you, let us just say that we'll be relocating soon. Jack is procuring a larger vehicle at this moment. Webb!"

The man appeared immediately. He must have been waiting just outside the door.

Graham picked up my derringer and turned it over in his hands. He released the catch and flipped up the chambers. "Loaded, of course," he murmured. "My, my, we are efficient, aren't we, Miss Hamilton?"

I watched him silently.

He latched it shut, put the safety on, and held it handle side out to Webb. "Use this to kill Kendall. Have your wife move the young ladies first." He raised a mocking eyebrow in my direction. "We cannot have their delicate sensibilities outraged."

"They have been sufficiently outraged for a lifetime," I croaked. I gripped the chair arms hard to keep myself upright. *Not Phillip. And with my gun.*

Webb was leaning past me to reach for the weapon. *Now or never.*

As he took the gun and pivoted toward the door, I stuck out my leg. He sprawled to the floor, the gun clattering out of his hand and skidding away. I ran, scooped it up, and was out the door in a moment. I whipped the door shut, turned the key that stood in the lock, and took it with me. What's sauce for the goose is sauce for the gander, as they say.

I'd have to hurry. Jack could return any minute, and Mrs. Webb was bound to hear the commotion. And if the shotgun was at hand...I ran for the basement.

As expected, the padlock on the door was still snapped in place, and no key. "Phillip! Claudine! Anna!" I called.

I heard muffled exclamations from the other side.

"Stand back from the door." I pointed the derringer close to the rusted bolt. It broke apart in a single shot.

The metal of the hasp was hot to the touch as I pulled it off, wincing, and flung open the door. "Hurry."

The four of us had gained the foyer—rushing past the pounding and shouts coming from the parlor door—when we heard the icy-cold voice of Mrs. Webb. "Stop!" She had just emerged from the kitchen and was advancing toward us, shotgun raised, Claudine in her sights. Kendall crossed protectively in front of the girl.

I pointed my gun—woefully mismatched as it was—at Mrs. Webb as she closed in, only five yards away now. "*No*," I said. "You drop *your* weapon and stand back."

Although she had the greater firepower, I saw her hesitate, lowering the barrel just a bit.

I pressed my advantage. "You are not a cold-blooded killer, Mrs. Webb. Let us go."

But the men could hear our exchange on the other side of the parlor door. Webb was calling to his wife now. "Mary! Mary!"

She bit her lip and raised her weapon again, putting her eye to the sights.

I had never shot a person...a *woman*...before. I almost closed my eyes as I pulled the trigger, as I had the first time I'd shot a grouse as a girl and had only wounded it. Papa's voice echoed in my mind—*eyes wide open...eyes wide open...* I had only one bullet left. I had to make it count.

Eyes wide open, I saw her drop. The shotgun blast went wide, raining ceiling plaster down upon our heads as we ducked and ran out the door.

Neighbors, roused from their beds by the sound of gunfire, were already hurrying out of their houses by the time we gained the driveway. There was no sign of Jack Porter or a vehicle. I could hear the rattle of wheels coming down the road at high speed, but to my immense relief, it was the sound of several conveyances. Help had come at last.

A police wagon and another carriage, containing Senator Cullom and Lydia Engels, pulled up to the house. And so the exhausting job of sorting out people and relating the events of the night began.

Fortunately, one of the neighbors—a middle-aged widow, of

the efficient, motherly breed—wrapped the girls in afghans and invited them to retire to her spare bedroom until needed. She had to coax the senator, however, to relinquish his hold on Claudine.

The widow also opened up her drawing room to the rest of us and plied us with hot tea and another pile of afghans—how did one person come to possess so many?

I was grateful to be away from the scene. I never wanted to lay eyes on Webb, Porter, or Graham again, and the thought of viewing Mrs. Webb—was she even alive?—chilled me to the bone.

Without a care for propriety, Kendall sat beside me on the settee and held my hand the entire time as I huddled beneath the layers of gaily colored, knitted throws. More than anyone, he understood how I was feeling. Lydia waited with us, not even raising an eyebrow at the sight of us holding hands.

"Do you know what happened to Hattie?" I asked her. "Is she back at home now?"

She nodded. "Mrs. Kroger is giving her the royal treatment. The senator said his clerk had kept the poor child waiting for an hour before going to get him. The man thought it was some sort of prank."

I blew out an exasperated breath.

Lydia's mouth quirked. "I understand the clerk got quite a dressing-down, right in front of Hattie, no less. That must have been a sight to see."

We heard the fading sound of carriage wheels heading for the street as Senator Cullom stepped into the drawing room. "The police have taken Graham and Webb into custody." He met my eye and shook his head. "The idea of Graham being involved never occurred to me. I'd been so sure it was Huntington."

"You can believe that Graham is still going to try to involve him and say he was simply carrying out Huntington's own plan." Not that I was concerned about the welfare of either man. Something else was on my mind. "What about—" I swallowed.

"Porter?" Cullom finished. "No sign of him."

I can take care of me'self. Never worry 'bout that, Jack had said. I had no doubt that he could. "Actually, I meant...Mrs. Webb. Is she dead?"

Cullom's eyes softened in pity. "I'm sorry. Yes."

Kendall squeezed my hand and looked up. "Pen had no choice, sir. The woman was ready to kill Miss Pelley."

Cullom nodded. "I know." His eyes met mine. "I am in your debt."

EPILOGUE

TUESDAY, JANUARY 25, 1887

*C*laudine, Anna, and I climbed the steps to the ladies' viewing gallery to observe the Senate proceedings. The young ladies were dressed in their finest walking suits and talked in excited whispers, eyes alight as if they had not a care in the world. Only Anna's short hair peeking beneath her bonnet was a reminder of their ordeal. The resilience of youth is enviable.

The police had found the rest of her snipped ringlets and her other evening glove wrapped in one of Huntington's monogrammed handkerchiefs. No doubt Jacob Graham planned to leave it behind to incriminate the man. The house had been rented in Huntington's name as well.

A week had passed since our rescue, and there had been some progress in unraveling the extent of the scheme. Graham had tried to assert it was Huntington's plan to kidnap the girls, but once a grief-stricken Webb unburdened himself to the police, the jig was up for Graham. Jack Porter's vehicle had been found abandoned near the B&O Railroad depot, but no sign of the man. I wondered if they would ever find him.

An additional bit of evidence against Jacob Graham came from the Pinkerton home office, where Frank had delved further into Crill's background. He discovered that Graham and Crill had known each other while Crill was active in the Tracey gang in Richmond, years ago—Frank promised to share his full report when I returned—and it was Graham who'd arranged for the Chicago charges against Crill to be dropped back in December.

He owed me a favor, Graham had said.

To Graham, December must have seemed the ideal time to put his scheme in place. The railroad bill was looking more and more likely to pass, and Huntington's opposition to it had reached a fevered pitch. Leonard Crill back in Chicago needed to evade a burglary charge. The senator's grandniece lived within easy reach of Crill.

With the services of an accomplished second-story man at his disposal, Graham could keep track of Claudine and give the word whenever he was ready for her to be taken. He slipped an anonymous note in Cullom's book and began plotting other ways to implicate Huntington.

However, when Claudine abruptly came to Washington, Graham had to adjust the plan. But that change worked in his favor, as he could then oversee things himself. I had thought Webb was the one who lured Anna away at the gallery, but it had been Graham. Jack and Webb had quickly sedated the girl, once Graham had her out of sight of the crowd, and tucked her into their pre-arranged hiding place.

I shook my head. A most unsavory man. Which of Collis Huntington's holdings had he wanted? Webb didn't know enough of the plan to say. Ownership of the C&O Railway, perhaps? *It's more efficient to have a hand in how one is supplied*, Cullom had said. But I suspected Graham wanted more than efficiency. He'd wanted it all.

We had the ladies' gallery completely to ourselves. Across the way, there were a number of men in the general gallery, heads bowed as the chaplain led the chamber proceedings with a prayer. We slipped quietly into seats just in front of the railing, where our view was unobstructed.

"Look, there's Uncle Shelby," Claudine whispered. Senator Cullom was standing before the dais to address his colleagues, accompanied by another man. "What's he doing?"

I tipped my head to listen. "He's formally introducing Mr. Farwell, the Senator-Elect from Illinois. I remember now. Mr. Farwell is replacing Mr. Logan, who passed away last month."

We watched Mr. Farwell take the oath of office, and both gentlemen resumed their seats.

It was a busy session. Credentials, petitions, bills, and resolutions were presented, read, referred, and filed. They reflected a dizzying array of interests—memorials for distinguished colleagues, bayou and river improvements in New Orleans, District of Columbia suffrage for the regulatory issues of its citizens…it was hard to keep track of them all.

Claudine shifted restlessly. "When will they be signing Uncle's bill?"

I shrugged. "I don't know. *You* wanted to come, my good miss. Now, stop squirming."

She shot me a look but settled down.

Finally, they reached the time when messages from the House were read aloud. "The Speaker of the House," the clerk said, "has signed the following enrolled bills."

Claudine leaned closer to the railing for a better look.

The President *pro tempore*, Mr. Sherman, picked up his pen and reached for the stack of bills to sign. I looked over at Cullom, seated in the front semi-circular row of desks. Cullom sat back with a sigh of satisfaction, then looked up over his shoulder in our direction. I lifted my hand in a discreet salute. He smiled before turning back.

As we left the ladies' reception room, we saw Phillip Kendall and Collis P. Huntington in conversation. Kendall's face brightened, and he strode towards us. "Congratulations are in order for your uncle, Miss Pelley," he said. "He worked long and hard to get that commerce bill passed."

"Thank you, Mr. Kendall." Claudine looked past him as Huntington approached. "Though not all feel that way, I expect."

Huntington took the girl's gloved hand and bowed over it. "Miss Pelley. I am glad you are safe. I regret my inadvertent role in the matter, in recommending the Webbs to your great-uncle. I had no idea there was a scheme in place to cause harm to you and your friend."

She withdrew her hand. "I appreciate the sentiment, sir." Her tone was neutral, though I, at least, could detect a chill.

He turned to me. "I have already conveyed my thanks to Mr. Kendall, but I wanted to express my gratitude for your efforts in clearing up the matter, Miss Hamilton. You have saved me from potential disaster."

I inclined my head. "You would do well to be wary of such men in the future, sir."

A tight smile froze on his face. "Indeed." He quickly excused himself and left.

"I'm surprised to see you here," I said to Kendall, who eyed the girls. They grinned and moved to a discreet distance.

"We've had no chance," he said, voice lowered, "to talk about what Lydia confided to you last week."

My lips twitched. "True. Certain distractions presented themselves."

"Well?" he said impatiently. "How do we stand, Pen? Am I still a thief and a liar in your eyes?"

I chose my words carefully. "Let us say I am relieved to learn that your...*irregular* activities had a more worthy purpose." Sometimes—just sometimes—the ends justified the means, though I wasn't ready to embrace such an ideology wholeheartedly.

His boyish grin returned. "Sort of like Robin Hood, don't you think?"

I grimaced. Stealing from blackmailers to give back to adulteresses was not exactly stuff of legend. "How long have you been doing this? I would not have thought there was much call for this sort of...specialty."

"You'd be surprised. I am asked to handle all sorts of matters, besides those stemming from *affaires de coeur*. There are occasions when due process will not achieve a just result. A different approach is needed."

"How does one advertise such a talent? Surely you don't post ads in the *Services Offered* columns."

"Now you are mocking me," he said.

I felt the flush creep up my cheeks. "Perhaps a little. It seems a rather hazardous occupation."

He looked at me intently, his eyes softening. "You *care* about my welfare."

"You cared about mine *first*," I retorted.

He laughed. "Fair enough. When do you head back to Chicago?"

"Tomorrow. The girls are returning with me." The danger to Anna's family had passed, the district attorney having failed to uncover concrete evidence that the Zaleskis had ever been involved with the anarchists in the Haymarket affair.

He raised an eyebrow. "Willingly? Miss Pelley is returning to the boarding school she complained of?"

"No, *not* the Chicago Ladies' Academy, but one that Cullom himself has inquired into. He assures her it will be better suited to her...temperament."

A smile played on his lips. "I can only imagine the curriculum of such an institution."

I had to agree. I wondered idly if they would be climbing trees and learning to tackle criminals. No, probably not. I hoped, at least, the school would teach the basics of ladylike behavior. Claudine had some progress to make in that regard. It is important to know the rules before one breaks them.

"Anna will be attending along with Claudine," I said. "Mr. Cullom has decided to pay for her education."

I remembered the senator's explanation at the time. "She was supposed to be Claudine's companion on this trip, not abducted in her place and used as a lure. It is the least I can do to make up for her dreadful experience."

A man of honor, if there ever was one.

I realized we had subsided into an awkward silence. "What about you?" I asked. "Are you returning to New York soon?"

He nodded. "There's a young heiress with a bit of a gambling problem. Lost her diamond necklace in the process..." He stopped and cleared his throat. "Well, the less said, the better."

"Be careful."

"I always am." He took my hand—his warm, slim-fingered grip was surprisingly strong—and lifted it to his lips. "Goodbye. And Pen..." He cleared his throat and continued, a catch in his voice, "Can you stay out of trouble for a while?" He abruptly dropped my hand and turned away.

I watched him walk out of the building without a backward glance. "I always *try*."

THE END

RESEARCH

~

I hope you enjoyed the story. This particular plot called for in-depth research into various aspects of 1880s life: railway travel, the city of Washington, DC, the passage of the Interstate Commerce Act (ICA), the history and layout of the Corcoran Gallery of Art (now the site of the Renwick Gallery), the architecture of the Senate Chamber, and the manner in which congressional proceedings were conducted, to name only some.

I also researched the life of Senator Shelby Moore Cullom, a real person I used fictitiously in this mystery. He was indeed instrumental in the framing and passage of the Interstate Commerce Act. This bill was the first piece of federal legislation to regulate railroad commerce and remedy the limitations of what states themselves could do. The following list (with commentary) contains the databases, sites, and indexes I used, should any of my readers wish to learn more.

Thanks for reading!

~K.B. Owen, July 2018

~

Primary and Secondary Sources

Books:

American Louvre, a History of the Renwick Gallery Building. Charles J. Robertson. Smithsonian American Art Museum, 2016.

~~My primary source of information about the original Corcoran Gallery of Art, now the site of the Renwick Gallery. As explained in the story, the building was taken over by the US government during the Civil War and used by the Quartermaster General, although I employed certain elements fictitiously.

50 Years of Service, personal recollections of Shelby M. Cullom, senior United States Senator from Illinois. Shelby Moore Cullom. A.C. McClurg & Co, 1911.

~~Invaluable source for Cullom's own account of his efforts and speeches regarding the passage of the ICA.

Websites:

railroads.unl.edu ~~1887 railway timetables

LOC.gov ~~Library of Congress digitized archives

ourdocuments.gov ~~digital copy of the original ICA document

HathiTrust.org ~~Congressional indexes regarding the passage of the ICA

govinfo.gov, The Congressional Record. ~~accounts of the 49th Congress, 2nd session, particularly the day the ICA was enrolled in the Senate

ChroniclingAmerica.loc.gov, a digitized database of historic American newspapers

nps.gov, the National Park Service website ~~historic district information for Logan Circle, formerly called Iowa Circle, in Washington, DC

Senate.gov (history sections) ~~directory of congressmen and chamber map of the Senate floor, which enabled me to determine exactly where Senator Cullom's desk was located. The site also provided sketches of the ladies' viewing gallery, reporters' gallery, general gallery, and other spaces

History.house.gov ~~accounts of gathering spaces in the Capitol and a timeline of renovations

ghostsofdc.org, Ghosts of DC, the lost and untold history of Washington, DC, a blog by Tom Cochran ~~historical maps of Washington, DC, photographs, etc.

househistoryman.blogspot.com, The House History Man, a blog by Paul K. Williams ~~information about the houses of Logan Circle/Iowa Circle

Streetsofwashington.com, Streets of Washington, a blog by John DeFerrari ~~historic pictures and postcards, hotel histories

https://youtu.be/CJy6IoODdg8 ~~Youtube video demonstrating the double-barrel Remington in action, courtesy of Mike Beliveau, historic gun aficionado

SPECIAL THANKS TO:

Barbara Bair, librarian at Library of Congress, who directed me towards HathiTrust and Congressional Record Indexes.

The law librarian, Law Library of Congress, who directed me toward the relevant congressional records of the passage of the ICA.

ALSO BY K.B. OWEN

ABOUT THE AUTHOR

K.B. Owen taught college English at universities in Connecticut and Washington, DC and holds a doctorate in 19th century British literature. A long-time mystery lover, she drew upon her teaching experiences in creating her amateur sleuth, Professor Concordia Wells and from there, lady Pinkerton Penelope Hamilton was born.

Contact:
kbowenmysteries.com
contact@kbowenmysteries.com

The Case of the Runaway Girl
The Chronicle of a Lady Detective
Copyright © 2018 Kathleen Belin Owen

Published in the United States of America

~

Cover design by Melinda VanLone, BookCoverCorner(dot)com

~

ISBN-13: 978-1-947287-00-6

Made in the USA
Middletown, DE
19 January 2022

59125951R00109